His desperation was breaking her heart.

Bert lifted his hand and softly stroked her hair. A smile shone through but Marcy was unable to return it. His black-fringed eyes filled with moisture as he gazed down at her. "Oh, Little One. It's been so long."

The next thing Marcy knew, she had both arms locked around his neck. The scent of leather, the strength of his sinewy shoulders, the unevenness of his breathing overpowered her senses. She had no idea how long she had clung to him, but she suddenly became aware that he no longer returned her embrace. At that moment, he placed his fingers securely around her waist and pushed her away from him. His motions were not rough, but they were firm.

Marcy was dumbfounded. Guilt, embarrassment, puzzlement churned inside her. Still her eyes were riveted to his face.

"I—I have to get back," he rasped, blinking rapidly as he reached for the reins. He swung effortlessly into the saddle and disappeared down the beach at a hard gallop.

JOURNEY TOWARD TOMORROW

Karyn Carr

Serenade/Serenata
BOOKS
of the Zondervan Publishing House
Grand Rapids, Michigan

JOURNEY TOWARD TOMORROW
Copyright © 1985 by The Zondervan Corporation
1415 Lake Drive, S.E.
Grand Rapids, Michigan 49506

ISBN 0-310-46912-0

Designed by Kim Koning

Printed in the United States of America

85 86 87 88 89 90 91 / 10 9 8 7 6 5 4 3 2 1

CHAPTER 1

MARCY DELANEY SETTLED INTO THE BACK SEAT of the big-wheeled Bronco, the only passenger. At first it felt a little odd being chauffeured, but then she decided it was just as well. Sitting up front beside her cowboy driver would have made her responsible for polite conversation, and all she wanted to do was start soaking up Florida.

"Welcome to the Sunshine State," the driver said, as they lurched into traffic. "My name is Nicholson Greer, and I'm foreman on the Coquina Ranch. Everybody calls me Nickle—nobody's ever gotten around to shortening it all the way to Nick—and that goes for you, Miss DeLaney."

"Then you must call me Marcy," she answered courteously.

"We have about a forty-five minute drive, so I thought I'd tell you a little about the ranch," he said, adjusting his battered straw hat. "It is twelve miles from town, we run three hundred head of Santa Gertrudis cattle, and raise Appaloosa horses. The present owner inherited it two years ago, after managing it for the last four years before the old man died. It used to be a year-round dude ranch, but now it's just open four times a year. We have eight hundred forty acres and a lot of beach front."

He had a deep, pleasant, almost professional-sounding voice, but Marcy's hopes for a quiet trip were fading.

"I'm sure I'll enjoy it very much," Marcy offered, hoping she didn't sound like it was an effort to be polite.

"I'm sure you will, ma'am."

The driver's speech was apparently finished, ending as abruptly as it had begun. The silence she yearned for was hers, and she gazed appreciatively at the Florida countryside dashing past her window.

Marcy had chosen a month-long vacation at the Coquina Ranch for several reasons. She had been a horse fancier and a good rider throughout her childhood and youth, and missed being around horses these last few years. Trail riding in soft sea breezes beckoned to her like the mythical Sirens luring helpless mariners. She was also a great rodeo fan and had timed her visit to coincide with the ranch's annual championship rodeo. The rowdy glamor of a rodeo always filled her with a wild, childlike excitement. She was going to devote one whole month to doing what she enjoyed most, and shedding the disappointment of the last few weeks.

Gradually the motion of the vehicle lulled away her tensions. The airplane trip from Atlanta was short and smooth, but the fatigue she hoped to peel off like a wet bathing suit was weeks, probably months old. She took a quick mental inventory: *I'm tired of wondering if I made the best choice. I'm tired of staying home doing the same old thing, going the same old places . . . and I'm tired of trying to get over Norman Powers.*

Norman. He stepped suddenly into her reverie as if they had stopped and invited him into the car. He was handsome in the way of Adonis, and a brilliant young businessman. At thirty-two, he was already president of a growing computer firm where Marcy had worked as his executive secretary. They had developed a warm, personal closeness inside the office and out. And though she had not pressed it, Marcy felt there was a future in their relationship; he had hinted at it more than once.

But the day the Board of Directors of the Corporation voted to elevate Marcy to a management position marked the beginning of the end for her and Norman. He couldn't even pretend to be pleased for her, she recalled. The promotion apparently made her a threat in Norman's eyes, a rival, and he became so uncomfortable around her, he stopped seeing her altogether. Within three weeks of their last date, his engagement to an Atlanta socialite was announced.

Marcy then decided the thing to do would be to remove herself completely from such a source of emotional discomfort. She not only declined the

Board's offer, she submitted her resignation. Norman's farewell was a pitiful mixture of guilt and relief. Although she deeply regretted that he was unable to share in the joy of her achievements and to be proud of her capabilities, her conscience bothered her on only one point. *How could you,* it nagged relentlessly, *simply walk out on such a career opportunity?*

She welcomed the cowboy's interruption this time. "This your first visit to Florida?"

"Oh, no. My aunt who raised me used to bring me down here to visit another aunt. We came for two or three weeks nearly every summer. I've loved Florida for as long as I can remember."

"Then you ought to be crazy about the Coquina," he replied, grinning into the rearview mirror.

They exited from the interstate highway onto a flat, straight road that stretched like a white ribbon into thick green pines miles ahead.

"Won't be long, now," Nickle volunteered.

Marcy returned her gaze out the window to the corridor oaks laced with Spanish moss. Thick, dark undergrowth had always represented a sort of sinister cosiness to her. As a child, she used to imagine what it would be like to be lost in such a place, walking on the deep carpet of leaves, peering through curtains of weblike moss. In her imagination, she was never frightened, just expectant. Behind what gnarled tree or from what swamp would the friendly alligator (who would turn into a handsome prince) emerge to take her to some magic kingdom buried in the woods' innermost depths?

She smiled at the recollection of her childhood fantasies, even though she had no handsome prince with whom to live happily ever after. Norman was handsome and princely, but in the final analysis, he hadn't measured up. Yet, whenever she squarely faced the facts, she had to admit that no one would probably ever measure up to her first real sweetheart. She had never again loved anyone the way she had loved Bert through her teen years. She had dated other men and made some good and lasting friendships, but maybe it was time to resign herself to the fact that, for her, the first love would always be the love of her life.

The memory that crept around her shoulders now was time-worn, and frayed around the edges. It was as comfortable and familiar as her favorite old sweater, and she felt it was a presence in her consciousness that would always be there. Actually weren't those memories some-how responsible for drawing her to an oasis of beaches and horses? She would always love the things they shared.

Before Marcy could lose herself in yesterday, the Bronco slowed, and she looked up to see a huge sign proclaiming The Coquina Ranch. They turned in under the archway of words and drove down a crushed shell lane lined with palms. Immediately after the turn, the dense under-growth simply disappeared, as if she had stepped into that magic kingdom of her dreams. Glorious-ly green pastures lay as far as she could see. Sparkling white fences divided and sub-divided the fields.

"It's beautiful," Marcy breathed. She presumed the red-brown dots way in the distance were the cattle. The horses nearest the driveway lifted their heads, froze their jaws in mid-munch, and pointed interested ears in their direction. Nickle rolled down his window and whistled. The horses who had not yet responded to their arrival swung their heads up to full attention.

"Oh, they're gorgeous!" Marcy exclaimed. "Could we stop here a minute?"

"Sure." Nickle eased the car over onto the grassy edge and turned off the motor. Marcy was out and standing on the bottom fence board before the engine died. Nickle walked up beside her and chuckled. "Can't wait to get your hands on them, huh?"

"No, I can't!" Marcy whistled low and steadily. "Come here, somebody," she begged. A bay mare eyed her suspiciously, and a young leopard Appaloosa was obviously torn between curiosity and reluctance. From farther out in the field, a red roan Appaloosa was walking purposefully toward them. "Come on, boy, that's it. Come on," Marcy urged.

The horse approached with confidence and accepted Marcy's eager petting willingly. "Oh, Nickle, he's marvelous." She looked into the warm round, brown eyes and admired the white blaze that traveled down his red face. "What's his name?"

"That's the Chief," Nickle replied, patting the horse smartly on the jaw. "Chief Joseph."

"Oh, then he's named after the Indian who rescued the Appaloosa breed, isn't he. Are you

12

that important around here?" The last question was directed to the horse, whose response was a nudge to the hand that had stopped petting him.

"I see you know something about Appaloosas," Nickle seemed amused. "We don't get many visitors here who know one end of a horse from another, much less any history of the breed."

Marcy stepped down from the fence and looked up at the friendly muzzle. "Do you have any Joker B blood here?" she asked.

"Well, I am impressed. Yes, ma'am, we most certainly do. I see right now I'll have to take you on a tour of the breeding barns."

"I'd love that! How about tomorrow?"

The horse sniffed her hair and snuffled softly in her ear. "You flirt," Marcy laughed, "I think I'm in love. Is he part of the riding string?"

"Not ordinarily, but I'll see what I can do about getting him for you. He's gentle and good-hearted, but he's a little sharper on his cues than our average trail horses. That can get greenhorns, uh, I mean, unskilled riders hurt as quickly as a rank horse."

Marcy laughed at his slip of the tongue and turned to see his gaze on her. She blushed lightly, gave Chief a farewell pat and suggested, "We'd better get on in. I'm dying to see the rest of the ranch."

After a final long, sweeping curve in the drive, there it was. The Coquina Ranch, which sprawled beneath the crystalline Florida sun, also offered cooling green canopies of palm fronds. The main lodge was of old Spanish architecture. The flaming bougainvillaea, which lined the walkway to the lodge, coordinated beautifully with its red tile roof. There were two hitching posts out front, and one held a small buckskin gelding. The horse nickered amiably as the cowboy got out of the car.

"Hello, Buck," Nickle greeted.

"That must be your horse," Marcy said.

"Yep."

Marcy's attention was captured by a horse and rider moving slowly through a small herd of cattle in the second fenced area from the lodge.

"Is that a pinto that cowboy is on out there?" She pointed toward the distant rider.

"Yes. That's the boss man, and a paint is all the boss man will ride."

A paint is all he will ride. Another one of those little coincidences that had become so familiar squeezed her heart. They occurred most often, of course, when she was around horses, because that had been their world together, their only world. For years she had been taking second looks at anyone on a paint horse. It had become second nature, so automatic she was hardly aware of it anymore. Bert was never there, but the schoolgirl who had loved him so deeply would always look.

The foreman's voice snatched her back into the present. "I have your luggage in the lodge, Miss DeLaney. After you check in, someone will take it on to your bunkhouse. It was a pleasure meeting you, ma'am, and I hope you enjoy your stay. If you'll excuse me, I need to get back to a little cow work."

"Of course. Thank you for picking me up. And please, call me Marcy."

"Yes, ma'am." Nicholson Greer was already in the saddle. He touched the brim of his hat to her, as he wheeled the buckskin away from the hitching post. She watched as they loped easily out of sight toward where she had seen the pinto.

Marcy took a deep breath and another long look around her. She grinned at the thrill she got from the earthy horsey aromas. "Coquina Ranch, I love you already," she pledged quietly, and walked into the lodge.

"Welcome to Coquina Ranch. You must be Marcy DeLaney," a young cowboy flashed her a lopsided smile from behind a polished oak counter.

"Thank you. Yes, I am, but how did—"

"You're the last guest to arrive," he interrupted, "Everybody else has already checked in." He shoved a leather bound registration book in her direction, "Sign here, please."

He can't be a day over nineteen, she mused as she signed her name. His lively eyes danced beneath the brim of his weathered hat. They were nearly all that remained in place on his distorted face. His right cheek was filled beyond capacity with a chew of tobacco. It gave him the appearance of a gluttonish chipmunk.

He noticed her studying him, and smiled again with the mobile side of his face. He leaned on his elbows and his voice took on a conspiratorial tone. "You'll have to pardon this, ma'am," he pointed sheepishly at his distended cheek. "I'm not supposed to chew indoors. I was out back

15

doing a little roping, and the boss man rode by and said, 'Cole, get on the desk, there's a guest coming in.' I'd just put in this chew, see, and I hated to waste it. I'm Jesse Cole."

Marcy laughed and offered her small, slim hand. "Glad to meet you, Jesse. Now where do I go? I think we'd better get you out of here before you choke."

"Just follow me," he said, coming out from behind the counter. "You're in Bunkhouse Number Three."

Jesse collected her suitcases and strode out a side door. He wasn't tall, but the large steps he took made Marcy trot to keep up. But then at five-feet-two, she usually had to move quickly to keep up with a fast walker.

She endured many nicknames pertaining to her size, but was rarely offended by them. "Half pint," "squirt," "pee wee" had all dogged her throughout her growing up years and occasionally in adulthood. Bert had had a nickname for her, and it was the simplest and sweetest of all.

Bunkhouse Number Three was at the end of a long path, and Marcy panted for breath, as she waited for Jesse to unlock the door. *Boy, am I out of shape*, she thought.

"Here you are, ma'am," Jesse said, as the door swung open.

Marcy stepped into the dark room. Jesse flitted about opening curtains and turning on lamps. "The air conditioner has been on all afternoon, so it ought to be pretty comfortable. The thermostat is right here on the unit. Make yourself at home, and if you need anything, just pick up the phone and dial 'one.'"

"Thanks, Jesse," Marcy said warmly. She took a dollar out of her shoulder bag and offered it to him.

"Oh, no thanks, ma'am," he refused politely. "No tipping is necessary or expected, here at the Coquina. In fact, it isn't allowed. Enjoy your stay."

As he left, she stepped outside and studied her new quarters. The cabin's exterior was of beautifully weathered cypress. It was situated in a sort of cul-de-sac, the only one on that path. Marcy was grateful for the seclusion; she needed time alone to think. The moist Florida warmth seemed to bathe her from head to toe.

Back inside she inspected the combination sleeping-sitting room. It was decorated to look like a Western bunkhouse. Branding irons hung over a stone fireplace, and the walls were adorned with Charles M. Russell reproductions. A wagon wheel light was suspended from the ceiling and dominated the center of the room. A huge round rug lay beneath it, and to Marcy's delight, she discovered several scatter rugs were saddle blankets.

In her rush to take full possession of the cabin, she began unpacking hurriedly. First out of her suitcase was her Bible, which she lay on the bedside table. As she arranged her clothes in the drawers and the sweet-smelling cedar lined closet, she wondered about the ranch's owner, the one on the pinto. She was sure he had a name, but so far, all she had heard was "boss man." His employees spoke of him with what seemed to Marcy like a curious mixture of familiarity and reverence. He's probably married, forty-five-ish, and came here from a working ranch out West, she thought, then chuckled and decided she might never know anything about him, because he might not have anything at all to do with the guests. She remembered that Nickle had told her the resort used to be open year-round, and now the "boss-man" only opened it once a quarter. She imagined he was tough but fair, and all business.

I'll bet he doesn't really like the tourists, she wagered. *I'll bet he'd just rather not have his life interrupted by a bunch of us greenhorns.*

"This is getting out of hand," she said out loud and sat down at the dressing mirror. She began brushing her light brown, shoulder length hair, and thought of another man on another pinto. Her blue eyes gazed at a reflection that momentarily became melancholy. *He so loved my hair*, she remembered, that first love who seemed to alternate between a memory from ages before and a heartache begun just yesterday. *He had called it spun gold and touched it as if the delicate fibers would shatter in his calloused hands.*

"I must stop this," she scolded herself. "That rider has opened a floodgate of remembrances!"

She resumed brushing her hair and appraising herself with practiced objectivity. She had been called "cute" and "pretty," but she never was particularly preoccupied with her looks. "Mediocrity," she jokingly assured her mirror image, "is much less a burden than great beauty. Now, where is that overnight case?" she mumbled, glancing quickly around the room.

When she discovered it was not in the bathroom, it dawned on her she must have left it in the car. Hoping no one had moved the Bronco from in front of the lodge, she walked out the door and set out down the path.

The car was right where she had climbed out of it, and she found her overnight case still in its place on the seat. Relieved, she reached in for it. When Marcy turned to close the car door, she caught a glimpse of the pinto and rider jogging around the far end of the lodge. Her heart leaped into her throat. *It can't be! It can't possibly be Bert!* But those long legs in stirrups just a little too short . . . and that slouchy position in the saddle. . . .

Dropping her overnight case, she bolted down the driveway. As she rounded the turn at the end of the lodge, she saw a trail leading through the palms. No one was in sight. At the end of the trail, she found what she decided must be the rodeo arena. It was deserted except for a few milling steers with wrapped horns.

How could he disappear so fast? Her pulse was crashing in her ears like the percussion section in a symphony orchestra, but sanity was trying hard to reassert itself. "Just calm down, Marcy, old girl," she told herself. "All these horses, the romantic air of this place, it's all going to your head. That could not possibly be Bert."

Why not? her heart teased. *Stranger things have happened. You've kept an eye out for him for seven years, don't you think just maybe, someday, somewhere, you'll see him again?*

"Shut up, heart. Take over, head," Marcy

ordered, as she walked back to the car and picked up her overnight case once more. But the striking similarities made it impossible for her to give up the notion altogether, and she turned into the lodge hoping to find Jesse behind the desk or the foreman somewhere in sight. Neither was there. A man and woman and young boy were sitting together on a leather couch. A striking brunette beauty was leaning on the registration counter.

"Excuse me," Marcy approached the family on the couch. "Can you tell me the, uh, the name of the owner of this ranch?" she asked breathlessly.

They looked at each other and exchanged brief frowns of concentration. The man shook his head, and the woman said, "I don't believe I know it."

The little boy offered, "All I've heard is 'boss man.'"

"Yes, well, that's all I've heard," Marcy responded. She looked up and noticed the brunette staring at her. She almost repeated the question, but the young woman's demeanor appeared cold and forbidding, so Marcy changed her mind.

"Thanks, anyway," she said, and turned toward the door.

"Miss," the woman on the couch called, "is anything wrong?"

"Oh, no, everything is fine," Marcy answered, suddenly aware of how distraught she must look.

"We're the Winfields. I'm Elaine, this is my husband Ed and our son, Eric. Are you a guest here?"

"Yes. I'm Marcy DeLaney. Glad to meet all of you."

"Well, we're glad to meet you, Marcy. Now, you're sure everything is all right?"

"Yes, just fine, thank you. I'm sure I'll see you again soon."

A final glance toward the brunette revealed that the icy glare seemed to have melted into boiling hatred. Marcy decided her imagination was dangerously over-active.

She returned to her cabin. She brushed her hair again and pinned it in a twist on top of her head. She noticed how flushed her face was, and understood Mrs. Winfield's concern. *I get red when I'm embarrassed, I get red when I'm hot, I get red when I'm flustered*, she chided herself. She couldn't count the times in her twenty-three years she had been betrayed by what she called her neon cheeks. It was a trait she had hoped desperately to outgrow. She had to settle now for the coolness of the shower.

In a few moments the lukewarm water coursed over her bare skin, seeming to empty her pores of city pollution and travel grime. Tension and fatigue whirled down the drain, leaving her with a feeling of release and renewal.

Softened into a state of dreamy relaxation, Marcy wondered what the touch of love, real love, felt like. She had never given herself, any of herself, to any man, nor had she wanted to, not since Bert. And back then, it was out of the question, because he guarded her teenage purity as if it was a treasure. Through three summers they loved with a sweetness and innocence that still brought tears to Marcy's eyes. Yet, the affection they did express let her imagine, through his intense maleness and tender love, what joy awaited her in womanhood.

Well, here I am, she thought, as she turned off the water, *and I'm still awaiting.* She had feared, on several occasions, that something was really wrong with her. Did she not have the "chemistry" other women had? Was she being too choosey? Was she stupid to hold out for feelings she hadn't had since she was sixteen years old?

She knew the answers. Of course, her "chemistry" was normal. Refusing to hop into bed for less than a genuine love that touched two people's lives in all dimensions and was anchored in marriage was not being too choosey. And Christian principles were never stupid.

After toweling dry and carefully rubbing in a delicately-scented body lotion, Marcy pulled on a robe and consulted the calendar of events that was on the desk when she first arrived. There was nothing planned by the ranch for that day. The guests were invited to "explore and make yourselves at home." A get-acquainted barbecue was scheduled for the next night, but this evening meals were available in the lodge at regular hours.

Marcy decided on a pair of semi-new jeans, a pastel plaid vest top, and her walking boots. While she loved Florida weather, she was not a sun worshiper, and what little daylight was left she was going to use to check out the horse facilities.

The arena was still deserted except for the

steers, which were now eating out of large rubber tubs. She walked around the fence and into a long, low barn. As she stepped through the doorway, she stopped to better absorb the sights and sounds of equine contentment. The herbal sweetness of hay and the candy smell of molasses-soaked grain were so strong it was as if she had lifted the lid from a pot of some bubbling delicacy. A chorus of crunch, crunch, accompanied by the occasional whisper of a mouthful of hay being pulled from a rack combined to stir actual pangs of hunger in Marcy's stomach.

"Hello! I thought that was you," said a figure walking toward her from the far end of the barn.

"Hello, Mr. Greer."

"Please, ma'am, call me Nickle. I brought the Chief in for you, and I think he's just about through eating. Would you like me to saddle him for you? You can ride, can't you?"

"Oh, yes! Thank you! I may be a little rusty, but I've done enough of it to still have it here and here," she said, pointing to her head, and patting the seat of her jeans.

The foreman laughed. "That's where it counts. I'm not usually wrong about who is a rider and who isn't."

The big Appaloosa stood quietly for saddling.

"Is this the breeding barn?" Marcy asked.

"No, ma'am. This is where we keep the trail horses and the ranch hands' horses."

Ma'am, ma'am, ma'am, Marcy thought. *I know they're just trying to be nice, but I feel like a school marm!*

Marcy gathered up a handful of mane, placed

her foot in the stirrup, and swung into the saddle. The stirrups dangled a full six inches below her feet. Nickle spoke as he shortened them.

"Now, the Chief doesn't have any bad habits, he's just quick and responsive. My only advice is not to go to sleep on him."

"I don't go to sleep on any of them," Marcy replied, a little defensively. She petted the roan neck and, tucking her toes back into the stirrups, gently touched Chief with her heels. He promptly moved out at an easy walk.

"The trail that leads off to your right at the far end of the barn will take you to the beach. All the trails are well-marked," he called after her.

"Thanks again, Nickle," she answered over her shoulder.

They walked quietly through the dusky shade of the palm-lined path. "Oh phooey, Chief," Marcy said. "I meant to ask Nickle the owner's name."

The Appaloosa aimed his ears toward her voice, then returned his attention to the trail ahead.

"Isn't this beautiful, Chief?" she said, as she gently stroked the horse's shoulder. "You and I are going to watch a gorgeous sunset." She noticed as she leaned forward to pet him, he quickened his pace. She recalled Nickle's comment, and made a mental note to be especially mindful of her movements in the saddle.

Some other sound or motion caught the horse's attention. He lifted his head, looked toward the right of the pathway, and nickered softly.

"That's probably just some other guests,"

Marcy responded. "They're riding friends of yours."

His reply was a full-voiced whinny that was answered in kind from beyond the tree trunks and dense yucca growth. Apparently satisfied with the affirmation that there was, indeed, one of his stable mates nearby, Chief moved on quietly.

With a slight pressure on the reins, Marcy stopped her mount and stepped down. The trail ended on a sparkling beach, glowing red from the fireball sun just beginning to settle into the water's horizon. Gulls called raucously, as they searched for an evening snack. Wavelets were chasing dainty sandpipers who skittered nervously, as if trying to keep their feet dry. The salt-sulphur heaviness made Marcy feel she could grab a handful of air and squeeze a tiny puddle of ocean water onto the sand where she stood.

Smiling, she reached down and pulled off her boots and socks. The sand was warm and yielding beneath her bare feet. She strolled toward the water's edge, her horse following closely.

With all her senses adrift on the shimmering waves, she didn't notice a horse and rider approach. The Chief did, however, and repeated his greeting. Startled, Marcy looked up to see the pinto standing a few yards away, the tall rider watching her.

Once more, her breath caught in her throat, and her heart struck a drum beat that pounded her chest. That horse, that silhouette! *It can't be*, the denials began again. But as he stepped from the saddle and began walking toward her, she felt disbelief roll away like a mist across the ocean. After seven years of wondering, remembering, looking, but never really hoping, here he was.

She had to be breathing, but her lungs seemed to struggle for oxygen. Welded to the spot, she could only watch as he moved steadily toward her. It appeared to Marcy that the whole world was being run in slow motion. But then, finally, there he stood, three feet away: yesterday in a straw hat and Levis.

CHAPTER 2

SHE STARED UPWARD into his emerald eyes, still unable to move or speak.

"Hello," his voice was strained and husky.

"Bert?" Marcy answered, trying to keep from trembling. "I—I can't believe this."

"I can't either. How are you?"

"I'm fine. How are you?"

"Fine, just fine."

Small talk was vividly inappropriate, and the silence that settled on them now transmitted more feeling than their clumsy words.

"You've hardly changed at all," he began again. A ghost of a smile played briefly in the lines at the corners of his eyes.

"Neither have you." Marcy could only take his words and bat them back, unable to tame her own wild thoughts.

He took a step closer, the pinto looked up at him, unmoving with ears pricked forward.

Bert laid both hands lightly on her shoulders, and they stood, asking with their eyes questions that couldn't find voice. His hands slid down her arms and took both her hands. She felt again the rush of comfort, and safety she used to feel when her small hands nestled in his. The magnetism of his body pulled her toward him with a force stronger than she had ever fought. Every fiber of her being screamed to leap into his arms. She wanted to bury her face in his chest and stay there for the next seven years, as a kind of atonement for the last seven. *Hold me*, she longed to say, *hold me forever and ever*.

Bert lifted one hand and softly stroked her hair. A smile shone through but Marcy was unable to return it. His black-fringed eyes filled with moisture as he gazed down at her. "Oh, Little One." His desperation was breaking her heart. "It's been so *long*."

Marcy wasn't surprised to discover tear after tear chasing themselves down her face. It was a function entirely independent of her will. She didn't want to cry. She didn't mean to cry. But she was crying. He brushed away the tears with the back of his fingers.

"I—I'm sorry," she stammered.

"Don't be sorry," he soothed in a coarse whisper.

The next thing Marcy knew, she had both arms locked around his neck. The scent of leather, the strength of his sinewy shoulders, the unevenness of his breathing overpowered her senses. She had no idea how long she had clung to him, but she suddenly became aware that he no longer returned her embrace. At that moment he placed his fingers securely on her waist and pushed her away from him. His motions were not rough, but they were firm.

Marcy was dumbfounded. Guilt, embarrassment, puzzlement churned inside her. Still her eyes were riveted to his face.

"I—I have to get back," he rasped, blinking rapidly as he reached for the reins. He swung effortlessly into the saddle and disappeared down the beach at a hard gallop.

Marcy felt anchored to the sand. The beach noises came to her as if from an echo chamber. The laughing gulls, the suck and hiss of the tide seemed both distant and amplified. Finally, Chief nudged her.

She reached out and stroked the velvet muzzle. "Was it a dream, Chief?" she whispered. But she knew it wasn't a dream. Bert had been there. After seven years of thinking back to the way things were and fantasizing how they would be, Bert was there. And she had made a fool of herself.

"Marcy, you idiot!" she cried, and kicked violently at the ground. Her quick motion and the spray of sand made the horse shy backward.

"Oh, I'm sorry, Chief," she stroked his neck, then led him to where she had left her boots.

Why did I have to jump him that way? Where was my control? How did I know he even cares about me or what we had?

Of course, her dreams always had him loving, needing, and wanting her as much as she loved, needed, and wanted him. Since she had never really expected to see him again, she never dealt with the possibility that he might not share these feelings. Was that it? Did he not feel anything for her at all anymore?

She got back on the horse, and they ambled toward the barn in the twilight. "It can't be." There was a note of defiance in her voice. "It can't be that he doesn't care. At least he cares about how it used to be. He stroked my hair, used his pet name for me, and I'm sure he was fighting tears. He held me, took my hands, touched my face. . . ."

Marcy felt her eyes stinging and brimming again. She shook her head furiously and gritted her teeth. *You poor little idiot*, she thought again, and gouged the tears from her eyes with a knuckle.

"Whoa, Chief," she tugged lightly at the reins, and the big roan stopped. "I have to get my face straightened out before we get back, in case someone is at the barn." She dried her cheeks on her sleeve, smoothed her hair and sat up straight in the saddle. "Let's go."

At the barn Nickle greeted her with a grin. "Well, hello, you two. I was about to get worried about you. Thought maybe you'd run off with my horse. How did you get along?"

Marcy made a weak attempt to smile back. "Fine, Nickle. He's terrific. Thanks." She stepped down, handed him the reins and walked out of the barn.

Back in her cabin, she sat on the edge of her bed and stared into the deepening darkness. Her mind was still whirling with thoughts, feelings, questions. How unbelievable it was that they should actually meet again! There could not have been a more idyllic setting for the reunion. The romance of palm trees and tropical sunsets. The pleasure and companionship of horses. The excitement of a rodeo. Had she drafted the perfect circumstance under which to rekindle a flame, she could not have improved upon the Coquina Ranch. But the situation was far from perfect.

Marcy switched on a light and rummaged through her purse for her billfold. She lifted several photographs from a plastic sleeve and thumbed through them until she came to a cowboy on a pinto horse. She stuffed the rest back behind her driver's license, propped a pillow against the headboard and stretched out on the bed. The picture had been cut down to fit into the window. It was dog-eared and cracked from years of taking out and putting back, but the subject's boyish grin remained undiminished. His right leg was hooked around the saddle horn, and his western hat was pushed back from his face.

Marcy compared the Bert of then with the Bert she had just met on the beach. The youth was gone, the smile was gone. The jauntiness expressed in the picture did not fit the quiet, solemn man of a few moments ago. She gazed at the laughing eyes, the mischievous face and said, "Are you still there, Bert, or are you someone I don't know anymore?"

For the first time, Marcy emerged from her own misery long enough to wonder what hardships he might have endured over the last few years. I handled it all wrong. *Never mind, I have to get hold of myself,* she decided. But the photo in her trembling fingers took her memory by the hand and compelled her to follow.

Marcy was sixteen, Bert was twenty-four. He had run a suburban Atlanta stable where she boarded her mare. He had helped her polish up her riding skills, and she had shown a few of his horses. They slowly and casually drifted into each others arms and hearts.

Bert was a cowboy, a typical fast-living, punch-throwing, hard-riding cowboy. They were very much in love, but their relationship was based on a closely guarded innocence, and they thought, a closely guarded secrecy. When her strict, maiden aunt discovered the depth of their association, she sold the mare, moved to the other side of Atlanta, and forbade Marcy to ever be in contact with "that stable hand" again.

It was a bleak time in her life. At sixteen, she had no choice but to do what she was told. She knew Bert loved her, and that by staying away, he was doing what he felt was best for her. Within less than a year after their separation, Marcy learned through a mutual acquaintance that Bert had left Georgia. No one knew where he had gone.

Marcy stirred again and slowly shook her head. She felt like a captured grasshopper being wound up in a spider's sticky web of memory and misery. She wanted to lift it off, strand by strand, and return to her life of several hours ago. *It wasn't so bad,* she thought, *watching for him and wondering if I'd ever see him again. It wasn't nearly as bad as having a sunny dream turn into a cold nightmare.*

Reluctantly, she returned the photograph to its years-long lodging in her billfold. She moved unsteadily to the dressing table and began absently brushing her hair. As it fell across her face, she got a faint but tantalizing whiff of his aftershave lotion. For an instant, she dreaded shampooing, because then it wouldn't smell like him anymore. And that fragrance, that mingled male sweetness might be all she would ever have of Bert.

A knock on her door so startled Marcy that she dropped her brush. It hit the dressing table then clattered to the floor. "Oh my gosh, what if it's Bert?" she mumbled. After a quick check in the mirror, a pat here, a smooth there, she went to the door. She seized the handle and took a deep breath. She swung the door open and looked up into Nicholson Greer's beaming face.

"Evenin', ma'am," the foreman nodded and tipped his batter straw hat.

"Oh, hi, Nickle." Disappointment and relief waged war in her voice. She wanted Bert to come after her, but she didn't look forward to facing him after her outburst on the beach.

"Did you get your ranch information and schedule sheet?" Nickle asked.

"Yes, I have one here somewhere. I read it earlier."

"Well, I just wondered, because I notice you didn't make it to the dining room during serving hours."

"My goodness! What time is it?"

Nickle fumbled with two aluminum foil wrapped packages in an effort to see his watch.

"I'm sorry, Nickle." Marcy reached for his burdens and invited, "come on in."

"No thanks, ma'am, I'd better not. I smuggled you a little fried chicken and potato salad out of the kitchen."

"How sweet of you! Do you keep such close tabs on all your guests?"

"Not usually, but your absence was pointed out to me twice, and I was a little worried you might not eat at all. I thought maybe—"

"After my ride," Marcy interrupted, "I came in and stretched out a few minutes. I guess the time passed more quickly than I realized."

"I understand. This salt air will do that to you. I'll go, now. Hope you enjoy your supper."

Nicholson touched his hat brim and stepped off her porch.

"Just a minute, please, Nickle. You said my absence in the dining room was pointed out to you. By whom?"

"The boss man, for one, and Mrs. Winfield, I believe it was, said she had hoped you'd round out their table to a foursome. The boss man tells me you two know each other from way back. Small world, isn't it?"

"Positively tiny. Did Bert, your boss man, send you here with the food?"

"No, ma'am. That was my idea." He grinned and studied the toes of his boots.

"That's very thoughtful, Nickle, and I appreciate it. I'm sorry if my absence was a problem. I don't mean to appear antisocial. Was I the only guest not there?"

"No, Lisa wasn't there."

"Lisa?"

"Tall, brunette, short hair. You probably haven't met her."

Miss Dagger Eyes, Marcy thought. "No, I haven't. But then, I haven't met any of the guests yet, except the Winfields."

"That's what tomorrow night's barbecue is all about. By the way, will you be wanting to ride the Chief tomorrow morning?"

"Probably," she began. Part of her was skittish about a possible replay of her evening. the rest of her resolved not to let this episode ruin her whole vacation. "Yes. Yes, I will. What time will he be finished eating?"

"He'll be ready any time after 7:30 or so."

"I see. Well, I don't expect to be there early enough to watch him eat." She managed a weak giggle.

"Whenever. Good night, now." The foreman disappeared into the darkness.

"Good night, Nickle, and thanks again," she called after him.

She spread her supper out on the dressing table. She was a little chagrinned that asking a blessing for her supper was the first time in the last few hours she had thought of prayer. She had become so immersed in her own weakness, she had momentarily forgotten that the source of her strength waited to be tapped.

Oh, Father, she rested her face in her hands, *I'm sorry I didn't come to you in my confusion. I am so grateful for this place and the chance to spend some time here. And I think I'm grateful for meeting Bert again, but right now, I'm not so*

35

sure. Be with us, please, as we renew our acquaintance. Give me more control and good sense than I had tonight. Thank you for this food and the warm friendship I've already found in Nickle, Jesse, and the Winfields. In Christ's name I pray, Amen."

Marcy was surprised at the hunger awakened in his by the crisp, tender chicken and delicious potato salad. Nibbling developed into dedicated eating. She was feeling decidedly better, and looked toward tomorrow with growing anticipation.

If I see him again, I'll be a model of control and detachment, she vowed. *We'll discuss the weather and laugh about the good ol' days. I will be politely interested in his acquisition of the ranch, and he will inquire after my career.* She turned toward the mirror, looked herself squarely in the eye and commented, "My, haven't we gotten stuffy over the years?"

After preparing for bed she slipped between the chilled, crisp sheets. With the air conditioner off, the night sounds of the tropics floated about the room. Singing bugs, peeping tree frogs, and cooing night birds were orchestrated against the gentle percussion of the palm fronds' whisper in the soft breezes. After reading several Psalms and turning out the light, sleep dropped a filmy curtain on two figures riding hand in hand along the water's edge.

Marcy awoke refreshed. She enjoyed a pleasantly chatty breakfast at the Winfields' table, though it was made somewhat uncomfortable by the hawkish attentions of Lisa, whose position at a corner table put Marcy directly in her line of vision.

Why me? Marcy wondered, as Lisa seemed to be dawdling endlessly over a cup of coffee and slice of toast, rarely taking her eyes off Marcy. She tried again to blame the other woman's peculiar attitude on her own imagination. Maybe it was one of those I'm-only-looking-at-you-when-you-look-at-me oddities that happen between strangers from time to time. Marcy had done that before, and such episodes would usually end with a smile and a nod. Marcy doubted that a smile lurked anywhere behind that ivory mask.

Determined not to let her dream vacation be ruined by a creeping paranoia, Marcy excused herself from the Winfields. Before she was out of the dining room, she heard a voice calling, "Mr. Treece! Telegram for Tolbert Treece!"

Her first thoughts were that she hoped Bert wasn't receiving any bad news. Before she could wonder any further, Lisa leaped from her chair, upsetting a glass of water. She strode up to the messenger with long, graceful steps and snapped, "I'll take it."

The delivery boy, apparently beyond speech, thrust a clipboard at her for a signature. His appreciation of her beauty was about to make his eyeballs pop out from their sockets, and he was clearly disappointed when their transaction was completed. Lisa glided through the swinging doors and disappeared.

Marcy was forced into a silent admission:

Whoever she was, whatever she was, with or without personality, she was one gorgeous female. But, why did she accept Bert's telegram? Were they friends? Lovers? Did she go with the ranch or with its owner? Does she know who Marcy is?

With strange new puzzles and possibilities cavorting in her brain, Marcy headed for the barn. In the scenario she had built around her daydream reunions with Bert, it had never occurred to her to write in a part for another woman.

As she passed the arena she noticed a figure in the center of it. His back was toward her, but she could tell by the lopsided way he wore his hat it was the cowboy who had checked her in. "Good morning, Jesse," she called.

He whirled around, spun a big loop over his head three times, then deftly snagged the gatepost beside her. Pretending a great struggle, he grappled his way up the rope. "Good morning," he grinned, half of his face already wrapped around a golf ball of chewing tobacco.

Marcy glanced toward where Jesse had been and saw a bale of hay with an artificial steer head and horns attached to one end. "Practicing your roping, I see," she offered.

"Yes, ma'am. Rodeo's coming up, and I have to get to work on it. Me and Nickle, we team rope every year. I head 'em, and he heels 'em."

"This is an excellent place to practice. Are those steer I saw in here yesterday some of your roping stock?"

"Sure are. I dropped a couple of pretty good

loops yesterday, but the boss man won't let us use them much this close to rodeo time. Says he wants 'em to be fresh for the shows. But then, the ropers do, too. It's no fun trotting along behind an old steer who's trying to stick his head in the loop just to get it over with.''

Marcy laughed. "Do you and Nickle practice together here at any certain time? I'd love to watch you.''

"The truth is," the young man leaned forward and dropped his voice as if to make a highly classified confession, "Nickle hardly ever practices. If I don't keep after it, day after day, I couldn't rope the toe of my boot if I was sittin' on my . . . well, you get the picture.''

"Yes, I do," Marcy chuckled.

"But take ol' Nickle, now. If he never dropped a practice loop, it wouldn't make any difference. Soon as me or whoever has the front end, he just sorta pitches his rope down, and the critter dances his hind feet right into it. I've never seen anything like it. In the three years I've worked here, I've seen Nicholson Greer miss two loops. That's just out and out miss. If the header doesn't do his job, of course, the steer gets clean away." Young Cole shook his head in wonder.

"That's amazing," Marcy agreed. She liked Jesse Cole. "I'll let you get on with your workout. See you later." She moved off in the direction of the barn then turned. "Oh, by the way, do you know Lisa?"

"Lisa who?"

"I don't know her last name. I thought you might have checked her in. Tall, very pretty

39

brunette." Marcy prayed she sounded nonchalant.

"Do you mean," he leaned toward her again with that gleam of collusion in his eye, "that there is *another* gorgeous cowgirl on this ranch besides you?"

"Oh, you . . ." Marcy made a playful grab at his hat, but he ducked, and she grasped thin air. He trotted away across the arena, and she started once more to the barn.

"I can't believe he doesn't know Lisa," she muttered aloud, "since he was apparently desk clerk while we were all arriving." Then a stabbing thought occurred to her. *Unless she isn't a registered guest.* Was he being evasive on purpose?

The ranch foreman, leading Chief, met her at the barn door. "Good morning. Your horse is ready."

"Good morning, Nickle. So I see. Are you into mind reading these days?"

"No, ma'am. I saw you over there talking to Jesse, and I assumed you were heading over here."

"You assumed right, and I appreciate it. But really, Nickle, if you'll show me where everything is, I'll be happy to saddle Chief myself. I would enjoy doing it, as a matter of fact."

"That would be okay, I guess." Nickle appeared restless and preoccupied. "But I'll have to show you around some other time. The boss man just rode through to draft me into a round-up."

Marcy felt her heart leap at the possibility of

Bert's nearness, but she she ordered her insides to be cool and controlled. "That's fine. Whenever you have time."

"I had planned to take you through the breeding barns this morning, now this." He sounded genuinely disappointed.

"I understand, Nickle, ranch work has to come first. We'll have another chance." She suddenly remembered the telegram and wondered if he knew about it. Asking would require treading a fine line between innocent curiosity and invasive meddling. He knew that she and Bert knew each other, but Bert may have indicated their acquaintance was casual or unimportant.

She stroked the Appaloosa's soft muzzle with the back of her forefinger. Nickle handed her the reins, and she seized her chance. "When I was in the dining room this morning a messenger came in with a telegram for Bert. It wasn't bad news, was it? You know how we're all conditioned to think the worst when—"

"Telegram?"

"Yes. Lisa, uh, what's her last name?" Marcy paused.

"Calloway," he answered flatly.

Marcy breathed a deep sign of relief. At least he hadn't said Treece. "Miss Calloway accepted it."

"Miz-z-z Calloway," Nickle corrected, with unsheathed sarcasm.

"Oh, sorry," Marcy said quietly. She was about to ask him who she was when he snapped his fingers.

"The telegram, of course. That must've been

41

when he heard. No, no it wasn't bad news. It was probably from the Texas rancher who is coming this afternoon to look at a young bull and some heifers. Those are the cows we have to go bring in. Speaking of which, ma'am, I'm sorry, but I have to get going." He walked back down the hallway and came jogging out on his little buckskin. In the true spirit of Old West gallantry, which Marcy was beginning to take for granted, he touched the brim of his hat as he rode by her. He prodded the chunky horse into a gallop and sped away.

Chief Joseph frisked in eagerness and anticipation. "Okay, okay," Marcy said, "We're going." The horse stood quietly for her to mount, but at her first signal, lunged abruptly forward. Marcy grabbed the saddle horn, shortened her hold on the reins and settled him into a quick, springy trot.

She turned him down a pathway between two scraggy yucca plants standing like sentinels. She soon felt the horse relax underneath her.

I refuse to let anything ruin my vacation, she vowed, but there were niggling doubts. She had to admit that it was already marred. Marred by a disastrous reunion with the man of her dreams. Marred by the unspoken wrath of some strange woman. But it wasn't ruined, and she would do all she could to prevent that.

A few yards down the sandy path, Marcy pulled up to read a weathered wooden sign. Large, carved, red letters proclaimed "Little Everglades." Below smaller ones warned, "Caution, please read." What followed was smaller print still, with worn paint. Marcy had to ease Chief closer in to read it.

The Little Everglades trail is a beautiful, educational ride through a wilderness swamp largely untouched by man. The construction and maintenance of the trail is the only human interference in this area. Please respect nature's delicate balance here, and do not leave behind anything you bring, or remove anything you find.

This environment supports many reptiles, some of which are poisonous. For your own safety, stay on the trail at all times and do not dismount. Thank you. The Management.

At the mention of snakes, Marcy felt a shudder of revulsion ripple through her. She peered down the trail into a deepening verdant darkness. Some fleeting thoughts skipped through her mind. *Maybe I shouldn't take this ride alone. Snakes, yuk! It certainly looks beautiful. The Management—that means Bert.* She abruptly straightened in the saddle and squared her shoulders in defense of imagined dangers and unwanted invading thoughts. "Let's go, Chief," she said, and touched the Appaloosa lightly with her heels.

As her eyes adjusted to the heavily shaded daylight, the excitement of risk mingled with her growing awareness that very real hazards dwelled here. The trail was elevated, pumped up, Marcy supposed, and a log fence with posts driven into the wet, sandy muck bordered it on each side. She ran her fingers through a length of red and flax mane in front of the saddle. "Somebody would really have to try to wander off this trail,'' she commented. Chief paid her a moment's attention, then resumed his olfactory exploration of his surroundings. With nostrils flared, eyes wide and neck arched, he bore his petite rider farther and farther into the swamp.

Marcy, too, was breathing the pungent, heavy essences that hung damply in the air. Sharp, rancid emanations reached her from a nearby Cypress grove, where the huge, ancient trees rose in mute resolution against time and the elements. Feathery, yellow-green needles grew in spirals on spindly twigs. Below the polished, hollow knees, a vast, intricate root system meandered through the murky depths.

The earthy effluvium of decaying vegetation was mixed with the earthiness of renewed life. The air felt as stagnant as the sluggish water that crept in out of the grassy, weedy marshes. In spite of the calm, she caught whiffs of the sweet white water lilies floating on the black pond. She knew the blossoms had opened soon after daylight and would close again as sundown neared. She felt today, they had opened just for her. As she was usually moved to do during an intimate encounter with the wonders of nature, she offered a silent prayer of thanksgiving to the Creator of it all.

A sudden movement of the other side of the trail made her horse jump slightly. Marcy caught a glimpse of a snake-shaped creature gliding out of sight under a cypress log. ''Whoa, Chief,'' she said softly. As they waited, a brown pointed head emerged from the water. After a few seconds of motionless observation, a long, thick grayish body and tail followed. "An eel!" Marcy murmured, fascinated. It glided along the log, searching for food or the next appropriate hiding place. To her surprise, she noticed four tiny legs, seemingly too small to be of valuable service, but contributing nonetheless to its locomotion. It disappeared again, and she reined Chief back to the center of the trail and moved on.

The steamy atmosphere was beginning to press heavily on Marcy. She felt a stream of perspiration trickle down her back, and her shirt clung to her. The teeming swamp had enchanted her, and she was already anticipating her next ride through it, but now, she was ready for less burdened air and fewer mosquitoes.

They emerged gradually into more abundant oxygen, as the dense undergrowth fell away behind them. Marcy didn't notice when the fence ended, but she found herself on a dry, solid road winding through scrub pines that she assumed led back to the barn.

With a light tap of her heels, they moved from a walk into a brisk jog. The long, uninterrupted road was an irresistible invitation to try her first gallop on the horse she was growing to love. "How about it, boy?" she asked, as she leaned forward and squeezed with her calves. Effortlessly, the Appaloosa eased into a rhythmic rocking lope. Chief picked up speed and she checked him only slightly, to remind him she was still in control.

The warm wind whipped tears from her eyes and lashed at her flowing hair. Exhilaration churned within her like a boiling geyser waiting to erupt. As they rounded a long curve, Marcy saw the barn in the distance. At the same time, she felt the Chief surge forward, harder and faster, apparently eager for his feed box. Faithful to one of the basic rules of horsemanship—never run a horse back to the barn—she reined him in. For a few frightening seconds, it felt like the powerful animal had no intention of responding. But then, he yielded, slowed to a short lope, and settled reluctantly into an energetic walk. Marcy patted him on the shoulder.

The familiar pinto appeared from the far side of the barn with his rider slouched comfortably in the saddle. He was moving in Marcy's direction, but when he caught sight of her, he stopped. After apparently coming to a decision, he proceeded toward her.

"Bert," Marcy whispered. The fragile glass bubble of distraction in whch she had dwelled all morning shattered.

CHAPTER 3

HE RODE STEADILY TOWARD HER, rocking with the sureness of one who had logged countless miles and hours in the saddle. He didn't speak until their horses' noses nearly touched. "Hi."

"Hi," Marcy replied. She felt the color rush to her cheeks in hot waves. *Lord*, she prayed silently, automatically, *somehow, You've got to help me do better this time*.

He shifted uncomfortably and, involuntarily, so did she. They had to talk. They had to start over somewhere, sometime. Now was as good a time as any. She marshalled all her courage and control and began again. "Did the man from Texas buy your cows?"

The expression on Bert's face made her wonder if that question had been a mistake. His eyes narrowed as he leveled an intense gaze on her. She felt a river of words, questions, and promises tumbling over the rocks in her throat.

47

I was there when Lisa accepted your telegram, she wanted to yell. *Why did she do that? Who is she?* Marcy wanted to demand that he put an end to her miserable confusion and put a bottom in the black pit of doubt into which she had been falling since yesterday. Instead, she explained calmly.

"I was in the dining room when the telegram came this morning." He tensed visibly. "Fearing bad news, I mentioned it to Nickle, when I got to the barn. He just assumed it was from the man about the cows, because he had been told to go help bring them in."

Bert relaxed and answered. "Yes. He bought the ones he came to look at and fifteen more head besides."

"Good," Marcy tried to sound enthusiastic. Again, silence deepened around them like a rising tide. When he looked at her at all, he seemed to probe and search. Otherwise, he studied his saddle horn.

Determined, Marcy plunged in again. "Bert?"

His eyes traveled slowly upward until they locked into hers. The desperation she had heard in his voice on the beach was unspoken, but dwelled in the deepening lines of his face. His brows drew toward each other and upward in a silent plea. The muscles in his jaw rippled over teeth clenched tightly against words or sounds that might betray the struggle inside him.

Marcy explored his square, weathered face, an older version of the face she had remembered with love for seven years. She felt pain at his pain, but was perversely reassured by the fact that he did feel something. "I want to apologize for my behavior on the beach yesterday. I have no excuses. I've been pretending a lot for a long time, but that isn't your problem. I sort of let the dream take over for a minute. It won't happen again. I want us to be friends, if at all possible. I'd like to hear about how you got here, where you've spent the last seven years, what—"

"No need to apologize," he said. "I was pretty rude myself, running off that way. Of course, we can be friends. I'd like that. We do have lots to talk about. But right now, I have some things I need to check on. You going to the barbecue tonight?"

"I plan to, yes."

"Good, good." He had become matter of fact. "See you later then." The pinto leaped from a standstill into a gallop.

Startled, Marcy turned to see him ride from view around the sweeping curve he had just left. Did that mean he would be at the barbecue? She was alone once more with her speculations on what she read in his face and heard him say. He was so different, so vastly different, from the fun-loving cowboy she had cared for so deeply. And yet, she had peeked through his disinterested, preoccupied veneer and seen memories and desires that matched her own. Or had she? Was she looking inside this person for a man who simply didn't live there anymore?

Marcy was relieved to find the barn empty. With little effort she located the tack room, unsaddled Chief and put the gear away. She brushed him for a long time, trying to figure out

Bert and trying not to think of him at all. Was he running from her?

Both times he approached her, and both times he couldn't get away fast enough. If she had approached him, she could reason that he was running from her. As it was, she almost felt as if he were running from himself. But why?

"Well, hoss," she ran her hand over his warm, damp back, "I'm ready to put you up, but I don't know where you belong." She looked down the long row of empty stalls and tried to remember which one Nickle had gotten him out of. "You tell me." Marcy unsnapped his lead, grabbed his muzzle in a quick hug, then led him by the halter into the hallway. She released his head and kept walking until Chief veered toward a stall.

"Is this home?" Marcy asked, and opened the door. The Appaloosa ambled in, and began munching on a bite of hay. With one more pat on the rump, she left him to his dinner and was suddenly aware of her own hunger. It was almost two o'clock, but she could get a sandwich at the dining room. Then she had all afternoon free to prepare for the barbecue.

Marcy's decision about what to wear took more time and consideration than she was accustomed to giving clothes. She soon became aggravated at her own motives. She thought of dressing up, until she confessed to herself it would be in deliberate competition with the mysterious Lisa. Marcy was no female competitor, even when she knew whom or what she was competing with. And in this case, she didn't.

On the other hand, good jeans, nice shirt, and dress boots would be perfectly acceptable for a Western style barbecue. But for some reason, that idea didn't appeal to her, either.

She took one more visual tour through her wardrobe and decided on a blue and white, bandana print, shirtwaist dress. Casual enough to be comfortable, yet a little dressier than jeans. She buttoned the tailored bodice slowly, thinking her arms were a little too pale below the short sleeves. It would be dark outside soon, however, and wouldn't matter. She really must get a little sun while she was here.

Fifteen minutes was all she needed for her make-up. She leaned closer to the mirror and noticed with some impatience that the morning's ride had allowed her face to sunburn slightly, in spite of all the time spent in the swamp. Freckles lying in wait across the bridge of her nose were already darkening. She applied a careful smear of foundation across the freckle zone and smoothed out a dollop over a mosquito bite beaming on her forehead. A tiny bit of blusher evened up the sunburn on her cheek bones, a touch of mascara and a daub of pink lipstick.

She brushed her hair until it shone and was tying the matching blue bandana around her head, when an uninvited memory stopped her.

"You look like a little cowgirl doll in that," Bert had told her one afternoon, long ago. A bandana kerchief she had worn to keep her hair out of her eyes had blown off while she was making the winning run in a barrel race. She was tying it back on after a congratulatory kiss from

Bert. He held her hair up in back while she tied the knot and before letting it fall in place he whispered, "I love you." Then he bounded off to enter the two of them in a rescue race. She had thought she would burst with love for him.

Marcy fingered the blue kerchief. She folded it gingerly, corner to corner, as if rough handling would bruise the morsel of yesterday it had conjured. She laid it in the dressing table drawer and rummaged for two white barrettes. She found only one and was closing the drawer when the paisley kerchief challenged her.

"Wear me like you did back then," it seemed to taunt. "That'll get him."

But Marcy didn't want to "get him" by trying to recreate a past he had not even acknowledged. If he didn't want to remember, she didn't want to make him.

"Besides," she said, as she slammed the drawer shut, "I might not even like this Bert."

She deftly plaited two small braids and caught them at the back of her head with the barrette. She slipped her feet into thick-soled white wedgies, collected her purse, locked her bunkhouse door behind her, and set off toward the lodge.

All the guests were to meet there, then go by horse-drawn hay wagon to a chosen site on the beach. Marcy spotted the Winfields.

"Hello, dear," Elaine greeted her with warmth and sincerity. "You look lovely. Doesn't she, Ed?"

"Absolutely devastating," he enthused with a smile.

Elaine winked at Marcy who made a small curtsy and replied, "Why, thank you both."

Their brief conversation was interrupted by young Eric's shout as the wagon rolled into view. "Wow! Here it comes! Mom? Dad? The wagon's coming!"

"Such energy," his mother shook her head.

The large wagon clattered to a halt in front of the milling group. Nicholson Greer and Jesse Cole hopped down from the driver's seat to help the guests into the wagon bed. Four musicians were already installed behind the seat and were tuning up in a raucous medley of plunk-plunks, boing-boings, and screech-screeches.

Marcy was hefted into the wagon and thought hayrides are getting soft when they put in hay bales and drape them with quilts. But she had to admit it was somewhat more comfortable than the itchy, sticky hay. She had hoped Bert would ride with them, but perhaps he was waiting on the beach. Her hopeful attitude was dampened some by the realization that Lisa could very well be waiting on the beach with him. As she settled on a bale at the fiddler's elbow, he leaned toward, removed his hat with a sweep that would have shamed Sir Walter Raleigh and drawled, "Evenin' ma'am."

"Evenin', sir," Marcy returned.

A distinguished gray-haired gentleman clad in Bermuda shorts and knee socks shared her hay bale. "Hello, hello," he said. "I believe this is a get-acquainted do, so let's. I'm Edmund Percy." He extended his hand, which Marcy grasped.

She was immediately captivated by his British accent. "I'm glad to meet you, Mr. Percy, I'm Marcy DeLaney."

"Now, now, none of that 'Mr. Percy' rot. Call me Edmund," he said, and proceeded to introduce her to other couples riding in the wagon.

The Winfields settled at the back of the wagon, where Eric insisted on sitting, so he could dangle his feet off the edge. Nickle and Jesse sprang back onto their seat, and with a perfectly timed, "Eeeee-ha!" cowboy yell, they popped the reins, and the wagon lurched forward.

Edmund Percy slapped his knee and declared, "I say! They don't lack spirit or atmosphere round here, do they?" He was clearly delighted, and Marcy had to laugh.

"No, they certainly don't!"

The bass guitarist began a low, droning rhythm, barely audible over the clacking chains and creaking wheels. After several seconds of repetitive strumming, he began singing in a resonant baritone, "An ol' cowpoke went ridin' out one dark and windy da-a-a-ay."

Marcy drifted through the old Western ballad with a tinge of nostalgia. While playing in her aunt's attic years ago, she had unearthed an old record of Vaughn Monroe's rendition of it. She had played it over and over on an old console radio–record-player combination. There were other records, but she claimed this for her favorite mostly because he sang about horses. Her attention returned fully to the young singer, as he intoned the last line. "Gho-o-st riders i-in the sky-y-y."

After a hearty round of applause, the little string band began again with a sing-along, and at the first strains, a cruel-nailed finger poked Marcy in her heart.

"You are my sunshi-ne, my only sunshine, you make me hap-py when skies are gra-a-y . . ." Marcy tried to join the enthusiastic chorus, but the words caught somewhere on rough, raw edges and made her eyes sting.

They had stood, hand in hand, singing "You Are My Sunshine" the last time she and Bert had been together. At one point, Bert hooked a finger under Marcy's chin and tilted her face toward his. He didn't sing the words, but spoke them to her with heartfelt conviction, "You'll never know, Marcy, how much I love you. Please don't take my sunshine away."

Three days later, Marcy was restricted to her room, and ordered never to see Tolbert Treece again.

Marcy took a deep breath and sat quietly until the song was over.

She joined in heartily on "Dixie" and enjoyed the musicians' version of "Cool Water." They were just getting to the "quack-quack here, and a quack-quack there," of Eric's request, when the smell of hickory smoke and a resounding cheer welcomed them to their destination.

Surprised at the crowd, Marcy asked Nickle if all these people were guests at the Coquina.

"No, ma'am. They're neighbors and business associates. The boss man doesn't throw many parties, so when he does, he tries to include everybody."

Her heart raced slightly at the hope of seeing Bert there, but her voice continued calmly. "Are they actually cooking with hickory?"

"No, ma'am, again," the foreman grinned.

"They're burning whatever they could get their hands on. Florida isn't exactly the firewood capitol of the world. The boss man bought bags of hickory chips for 'taste and atmosphere.'" At the quote from the boss man, Nickle stiffened and inspected his fingernails in a gesture of mock sophistication mixed with disdain.

"Do you all like Bert?" Marcy blurted it out, before she realized what she was saying. Maybe, if she could look at him, even briefly, through someone else's eyes, she could gain a different perspective.

"We 'all' who, ma'am?" Nickle teased.

"That's not Southern talk, suh," Marcy retorted in her finest Atlanta drawl. "I mean all of you who work for him."

"Sure. What's not to like?" Nickle's expression became veiled, as if he were retreating behind a gauzy curtain of uncertainty to weigh and measure his responses. He turned away from Marcy and began unloading the musicians' equipment. As he headed toward the revelers, Marcy heard him mumble, "Until lately, anyway."

Unable to pursue her questioning, she joined the group that had formed a wandering circle around the barbecue site. The spit-browned pork had already been removed and cut into servable portions. Marcy was glad. She had always felt a little barbaric watching animals roast whole on a stick. She couldn't watch it without feeling that she was a reluctant spectator at a modern sacrificial rite. But the delectable-looking meat was bubbling gently in its spicy, sweet sauce in large iron cauldrons suspended above the flames.

Marcy spoke politely to strangers and talked absently with the guests she had met on the wagon. She scanned the milling crowd, partly out of a habit seven years old, and partly out of a new, compelling expectancy. *Surely he'll be here*, she thought. *He's the host.*

"Ladies and gentlemen," their attention was drawn en masse toward a makeshift stage constructed beneath a trio of palms. Marcy was again aware of the professional quality in the foreman's voice. "On behalf of Mr. Tolbert Treece, I'd like to welcome you to the Coquina Ranch. Mr. Treece owner of this fine little establishment," he paused for the ripple of laughter to dissipate, "was unexpectedly called away on business this afternoon. He sends his regret that he can't be here with you. He also sent explicit instructions for you to eat up, drink up and have a grand ol' time!" The rest of the crowd applauded energetically, but Marcy stood still trying to absorb Nickle's comment. *So, he won't be coming after all. He probably didn't intend to see me later at all.*

Fearful her disappointment was showing in her countenance, Marcy was grateful for Nickle's next words. "Now, if those of you who are of like mind will join me in a word of grace, we'll get to the vittles."

Marcy lowered her head quickly, but something in Nickle's prayerful soliloquy commanded her attention away from her unhappiness. She looked up at him, standing tall and erect, holding his battered straw against his chest. His eyes strayed heavenward and came to rest somewhere near the bottom edge of the azure sky, where it dissolved into a flaming horizon.

"Lord," he began, chin high and resolute, "we're cowboys and congressmen, wranglers and ranchers, bankers and brush-poppers, but we're all the same to You, and we thank You for that plan. You must've smiled when You laid out the Coquina, and we thank You for the good living it provides some of us and the good times it provides all of us. We thank You, too, for this food we're about to have and for all the people who have made this possible. Grant us a safe ride on the right trail, Lord. Amen."

A few murmured "amens" drifted to Marcy's ears, one of them from her own mouth. The cook clanged a dinner bell and squalled, "Come and get it!"

Marcy stood watching the lanky cowboy. He pushed a rough hand through his hair and slapped his hat down on his head in an effort to capture the unruly locks before they sprang once more to freedom. He stepped easily off the stage and walked toward where the buffet line was forming.

It's funny, she thought, how we form opinions of people, and then promptly have to start changing them. Suddenly, this "yes, ma'am, no, ma'am," over-polite, strictly business ranch hand had revealed a warm, deep, caring, grateful slice of himself. Marcy found it a little disarming. As he passed her, she touched his elbow.

"Thanks, Nickle, that was nice."

"Certainly, ma'am," he replied, smiling. He was Nicholson Greer again, foreman of the

Coquina Ranch, public relations man for the owner and keeper of the tourists' time and pleasure.

Marcy found the end of the chow line. Although she didn't feel particularly hungry, the spread of fried chicken, barbecue, potato salad, baked beans and corn on the cob was so inviting, she sampled all her plate would hold and looked around for a seat.

"Do sit here, love," Edmund Percy shifted to make a space for her between himself and eight-year-old Eric.

"Marvelous feast, this, eh?" Edmund asked between mouthfuls.

"Yes, it is," Marcy answered, anticipating her first bite of the succulent pork.

They ate in silence for awhile, each intent on devouring his or her portion of the sumptuous fare. Presently, Mr. Percy touched her hand to get her attention. "Marcy," he began.

Marcy turned to look into a kind face that had put on a rather fatherly demeanor since she had last noticed. His voice was quietly concerned. "Are you having a good time?"

"Why, yes. This is delicious."

"I don't mean just the food," he continued, "I mean this place, your vacation. If you don't mind my saying so, you seem troubled from time to time. And you're so, well, so alone."

Marcy laid her fork down and looked at him thoughtfully. She was accustomed to the uncomfortableness most men suffered in her presence. For as long as she had been on her own, they either took the posture of protector or assumed that she was on the prowl—for them, naturally. She had concluded it was impossible for a man to simply accept her aloneness as a choice or life's design, rather than a pitiable state. This vacation had been refreshingly void of such attitudes.

"Really, Edmund, I'm having a lovely time. And I'm hardly alone," a short sweep of her hand took in a number of diners. "Besides, I have lived by myself for several years and learned some time ago I could have as much fun with me as I could with anybody else."

"Well that's fine then," he said, "but as the saying goes, if I were a few years younger . . ."

They both broke into laughter.

The rest of the evening passed quickly. After the last plates were emptied of their desserts the musicians plunged headlong into a banjo breakdown. And Nickle announced it was time for everyone to get in the mood for "a good ol' hoedown." Moans of disbelief rippled through the bloated partyers. In spite of a universal conviction that no one could move, much less dance, there was soon widespread toe-tapping and hand-clapping.

Marcy determined she would enjoy the evening, and soon responded to the mirth around her. She square danced with various partners— Jess, Edmund, even the bass player in the band. The evening wound down with "The Tennessee Waltz," which she shared with Nickle.

Finally the musicians packed up instruments, amplifiers and microphones. Marcy watched absently as several couples drifted out to stroll along the water's edge, until Edmund gently touched her elbow. She quickly joined all the Coquina guests heading back to the wagon.

The trip to their quarters was made in silence, except for short periods of quiet, contented chatter. Eric was asleep on his hay bale in five minutes, and two honeymooners were huddled in a corner, as if fearful that a hefty gust of wind would blow them apart.

It had been a good party, and Marcy complimented Nickle and Jesse on its success. The drivers seemed genuinely pleased with the evening and commented that the boss man had missed one of the best ever.

The boss man. In the dark, warm, soft, still night, his image reentered like a naughty, wayward spectre. The good food and dancing had left her weary, and her thoughts of him now were casual and undemanding. She wondered if business had really kept him from his guests. She wondered if she was the real reason he had stayed away. And she wondered at the absence of Lisa Calloway.

When Nickle pulled the horses to a halt in front of the lodge door, Marcy noticed a silhouette leaning in the doorway. Guests were helped down, good nights were said, and the drowsy partyers scattered into the night.

As Marcy walked from the wagon, Edmund, Jesse, and Nickle thanked her in turn for her dances. From out of the blackness behind her, a low, sultry feminine voice charged flatly, "Belle of the ball, I see."

CHAPTER 4

MARCY SPUN AROUND TO SEE Lisa Calloway shimmering before her in a fluid, black satin evening gown. Trying to master her surprise and defensive feelings, Marcy did not reply to her comment. Instead, she stated coolly, "I don't believe we've met. I'm Marcy DeLaney."

"Lisa Calloway," the brunette snapped. She turned abruptly and glided back into the darkness and out of sight.

Marcy looked around to see if she were alone. Nickle, who had remained intent upon some problem with the horses' harness, looked up and approached Marcy. "Well, what do you think of her?"

Marcy felt totally disarmed and confused by the episode. "A chunk of spit-shined concrete," she answered tartly, and immediately regretted it.

Nickle laughed heartily. Knowing it was too

late to recall the words uttered in haste, she tried at least to soften them. "I'm sorry, Nickle. I shouldn't have said that. I feel catty enough to go lap up a bowl of milk."

The foreman laughed again. "Don't apologize to me. That's about as accurate a description as I've heard. And more charitable than most, too. I apologize to you for her behavior."

"You? What do you have to apologize for?"

"Nothing, personally. I just mean I don't like for one of my guests to be treated rudely, by another guest or anybody else. That's all. I'm just sorry it happened. Let me walk you to your cabin."

Marcy allowed him to steer her onto the pathway leading to Bunkhouse Number Three. "Is she a guest here?"

"Sort of."

"Is she that way toward everybody, or just me?"

"Everybody, mostly. She's pretty stand-offish."

"I didn't see how it could be just me, since she doesn't even know me. How can someone despise a total stranger?"

"She manages."

Marcy noticed how cryptic his answers had become. She didn't want to appear nosey or pushy, but the woman's behavior was undeniably peculiar, and she felt she deserved some answers.

They arrived at her door and stood, awash in the soft yellow lamplight. "Nickle," she began, unsure of whether she really wanted to hear the answer, "who is she?"

"Come on, now, don't worry about her. She won't bother you. She may not even show up any more. Even though she does coil up and hiss now and then, she isn't really poisonous. Just don't pay any attention to her."

Marcy looked up at Nickle, and something in his expression distracted her from her next question. Nickle's eyes held hers for a long, intense moment. They moved along her hairline, and traced a line to her lips. Then as if awakening from a hypnotic trance, Nickle looked toward the bunkhouse. "Would you like for me to unlock your door?"

"No," Marcy answered, thinking she must have misread his expression in the darkness. "I can manage fine. Thanks for walking me home."

"Sure." Nickle backed off the porch and tipped his hat. "Maybe we can work in that trip through the breeding barns tomorrow. Good night."

"Good night," Marcy called to the retreating figure. She let herself in and flipped the light switch. The room was a welcome haven after the last few unsettling minutes. She performed her bedtime preparations, busying her mind with the extraordinary Lisa.

She was grateful for Nickle's concern for her, and his attentiveness. She knew she should show more appreciation for him, although she realized no man could get the attention he deserved in any relationship with her as long as she was here with Bert.

But she wasn't *with* Bert, she admitted reluctantly. Was Lisa? Marcy couldn't rationalize

64

how a man who had loved her could be attracted to someone like Lisa. *We are so unlike each other*, she thought. Maybe that was it. The twenty-four-year-old who went for small, horse-crazy, blue-eyed blondes grew into a thirty-one-year-old who went for tall, beautiful, sophisticated brunettes.

He had loved her, then. Nothing would ever shake her belief that when they were together, he loved her strongly, deeply, and with dedication. Perhaps it was ridiculous of her to dare to hope he still felt for her what she felt for him, much less expect it. How many men would fan a flame for seven years, a flame that was lit by a child? Very few. But in her dreams, Bert had.

Sleep came easily and quickly. The night seemed to last minutes instead of hours, and the sun was shining brilliantly when Marcy looked out into the pristine morning. She slipped into a pair of khaki walking shorts and a sleeveless knit pull-over. She sped through her make-up regimen and set out for the lodge. *I hope these snow-white arms and legs don't blind anybody*, she thought.

Halfway through her breakfast, she was joined by Edmund Percy. He was a delightful conversationalist, and Marcy enjoyed his company.

"Are you going on the trail ride this morning?" he asked.

"I forgot there was one. I guess I'm not following my calendar of events very closely. When is it?"

"I believe we are to leave the barn around ten-thirty. Someone is supposed to take us tenderfeet out for a couple of hours. It is my theory that by the time we get back, it shan't be our feet that are tender!" He shook with laughter at his own witticism.

Marcy was more amused by him than by his joke. "I think I'll pass this one up. I'd like to spend a little time in the sun, and I'm so pale, it has to be in the early morning or late afternoon. Midday Florida sun would fry me. But I'm sure you will have a good time."

She returned to her cabin to change into her yellow swim suit, and a white terry cloth cover-up. She checked her watch as she pulled on her yellow sandals. Nine-fifteen. She would have to hurry if she got in much sunbathing time before the scorching rays became too much for her fair skin.

Once outside she selected a chaise and stretched out. No one else was there except the honeymooning couple she had seen on the hay wagon, thoroughly oiled and glistening across the pool from her. They held hands between their chairs and lay, eyes closed, drifting on their own euphoric cloud.

Marcy had a mild flurry of envy that was quickly replaced by wonder. Would she ever have those feelings? Would there ever be a man whom she wanted to hold constantly? Would there ever be a man who couldn't bear to let her out of his arms?

Heat and brightness poured over her relentlessly, interrupted only by an occasional cottony wisp of cloud floating across the sky. Marcy fidgeted. She sat up and lay down. She could never lie in the sun for hours like many of her friends did, but boredom was setting in sooner than usual this morning. Boredom? Was that really the source of her restlessness?

She vaulted from her chair and dove into the pool. She swam its length twice, then clung to the side, gasping for air. After a few more laps, she relaxed in the sun until her suit dried.

As she passed the lodge on her way back to her bunkhouse, she was overcome with hunger. I'll make a quick detour and grab a snack, she decided, and pushed open the heavy door. The air conditioned draft that met her was welcome. She perched on a chair near the kitchen entrance again, and asked if she could get food to take out.

"You sure can," the waitress said.

"Then I'll have a hamburger, some fries, and a small iced tea," Marcy ordered and handed back the menu.

She presumed the deserted dining room was testimony to the fact that the morning's trail ride was not yet over. She grinned at the thought of Mr. Percy bouncing resolutely along.

The kitchen door swung open and Marcy turned, expecting to be handed her lunch. Instead, she looked blankly into the faces of Bert and Lisa.

"Hello, Marcy," Bert spoke first.

"Hello, Bert," Marcy's voice sounded distant to her own ears.

"Have you two met? Lisa, this is—"

"We've met," Lisa interrupted crisply. "How are you?"

"Fine, thank you. How are you?" Marcy responded.

In the ensuing silence, Marcy became painfully aware of her disheveled appearance. A glance at Lisa's perfectly combed, shiny locks made Marcy reach up to smooth her own hair. With dismay, she felt a cap of wiry curls and tendrils that always sprang to life when allowed to dry on their own. Lisa's white shorts flattered her silken legs and complemented a red and white clingy knit shirt. Marcy's long, hooded robe, a poolside rage in Atlanta, suddenly felt like swaddling clothes. Lisa's olive complexion was highlighted beautifully. From the properly graduated blend of eye shadows to lips the exact red in her shirt, her face was a study in faultlessness. Marcy's face stung and prickled from the morning's sun, and she knew her make-up had not withstood the swimming and sweating. Essence of jasmine seemed to escape from Lisa's very pores, while Marcy whiffed nothing from herself but chlorine and Coppertone.

Adding to her embarrassment, Marcy noticed that Lisa's expression was not one of contempt or anger, as it had been during their previous encounters. Was it amusement? Ridicule? *What gratification is she getting from catching me at my worst,* Marcy wondered. *Is she enjoying my predicament so much because she is with Bert?*

The waitress poked her head out between the swinging doors and announced, "Miss Calloway, you have a telephone call at the registration desk."

Lisa turned without a word and stalked out of the dining room.

The waitress added, "Your burger will be ready in a minute, ma'am."

"Thank you," Marcy managed, wishing she could retreat from sight into the depths of her robe.

Bert touched the back of the chair across the table from her. "May I?" he asked.

"Of course, of course. Please, sit down. Where are my manners?"

"Did you enjoy the water?" Bert inquired, with the practiced concern of a tourist handler.

"I sure did," she replied. "It was delightful."

"Good. Are you going back to the pool after you eat?"

"No. I've been wanting to see your breeding stock, and your foreman said he might be able to take me through the barns this afternoon."

"That'll be nice." Bert studied the clock hanging over the kitchen doorway. He then returned his gaze to Marcy and contemplated her face, much as he had the clock's. Before he could share his deliberations, if he even intended to, the waitress appeared with Marcy's lunch.

"Here you are," she set the white bag down carefully.

"Thank you." Marcy glanced up at the young girl whose smile was strangely knowing. *I'll bet there are no secrets around here* she thought. *Everybody on the ranch probably knows we meant something to each other in the past, but they don't know under what circumstances.*

Bert interrupted Marcy's reverie. "I guess you'd like to go eat that before it gets cold." He walked around the table to hold Marcy's chair, then he walked with her to the door.

Fearful of saying the wrong thing, even for the

sake of polite leave-taking, Marcy refrained from telling Bert it was nice to see him. She was trying to come up with some sort of innocent farewell, when Bert asked, "You're riding Chief Jospeh, aren't you?"

"Why, yes, I am. Is it all right?"

"Oh, sure, it's fine. I okayed it, as a matter of fact. How do you like him?"

"I love him, Bert, he's wonderful." It was easy for Marcy to be sincerely enthusiastic when discussing the Appaloosa.

"That's great. I'm glad he's working well for you. Although, I wouldn't really expect anything else. He always works well with a good rider. When Greer asked me if you could use him, I thought that of all the horses on the place, he's the one most suited to you."

Marcy silently rejoiced. He *had* been remembering! "We did seem to hit it off, right from the start," she said.

"Well, enjoy your lunch," he turned from her and walked away in the opposite direction.

"Thanks," she called after him.

Walking to her bunkhouse, she tried to restrain her elation over Bert's remark, but was not entirely successful. She fed on it cautiously and as objectively as she could, but she sucked it dry of every last drop of innuendo. He remembered enough, in enough detail, to know instinctively which horse would suit her. Had he recalled other facets of their relationship with equal accuracy? If he remembered her preference in horses, wouldn't it be inevitable that he remember her preference, to put it mildly, for him?

Marcy was feeling hope again, if not hope for the realization of her seven years' dream, at least a little more faith in the authenticity of her memories.

After showering she blow dried her hair briefly, but was too excited to sit long enough to completely dry it. All too aware of how kinky it would become if left loose and damp, she planned her strategy as she dressed.

She dusted on some lightly scented lilac body powder and snickered at the pun she made. "I'll fight flower with flower," she resolved, remembering the jasmine-through-the-window-on-a-summer-night air around Lisa. Although she would be spending the afternoon on a horse with Nickle, she would make every effort not to get caught unprepared again. If Bert and the blossom-laden beauty were going to turn up any place at any time, she would just have to be ready.

Marcy stepped into an old but comfortable pair of jeans and pulled on her yellow Stan Brock "Help Preserve Wildlife" tee shirt. She plaited her hair into one braid down her back and tied the end with a blue ribbon. A blue bandana kerchief kept the escaping curls around her face in check.

Her face was next under scrutiny. A little mascara and a touch of foundation to tone down an ever-reddening nose was all she applied. Anything else would be wasted as her sunburn deepened.

She jammed her feet into her favorite riding boots, locked the door, stuffed the key in her pocket, and hurried toward the barn. What she really wanted to do was run. She couldn't wait to be with Chief, the horse that was her first real link between yesterday's man of her dreams and today's Bert.

The first thing she saw as she approached the barn was Chief's white-blanketed roan rump. He was saddled. Puzzled, Marcy called out, "Nickle? Are you into mental telepathy or something? How did you know that I was coming?"

Her only reply was a deep-throated chuckle of greeting from the Chief and a sharp snort from another horse. "Hi, buddy," Marcy said, petting her mount's head. He leaned into her heavily as she scratched his ears, and she noticed he was already damp under his bridle.

"How long have you been saddled, boy? Or has somebody else been riding you?" An unwelcome sensation of jealousy crept through her, when she spoke the second question. She had begun to think of Chief Joseph as *her* horse, and Bert's hearty endorsement of them as a team had heightened her feelings of possessiveness. "Nickle!" she shouted.

Still no answer. She ducked under Chief's neck, intending to check the feed and tack rooms for any signs of life. But her journey down the barn hall was ended abruptly, when she caught sight of its other occupant. There, standing quietly, inspecting her curiously, saddled and waiting, stood Bert's pinto.

CHAPTER 5

MARCY'S BRAIN WAS BOMBARDED with questions. Had Bert and someone on Chief been riding? Was it Lisa? She seethed at the very idea, but was forced to admit her anger and her claims on that horse were both irrational. He belonged to the ranch. Anyone who wanted to and was able could ride him.

She was about to yell for Nickle again, when she heard the feed room door slam at the far end of the barn. The figure striding toward her was not the foreman. Marcy's heart lurched, and she swallowed compulsively.

"Ah, you're here," Bert acknowledged. "I was emptying some sacks of grain into the bins, and I couldn't hear you come in. Are you ready?"

"Ready for what?" she asked. *That was stupid*, she thought, after the words were out.

"Weren't you planning to ride over to the breeding barns this afternoon?"

"Well, yes, I was, but I thought . . ."

"Greer isn't back with the guests, yet." Bert glanced at his watch and frowned. "I have some time and thought I'd take you over. That is, if it's okay with you."

"Okay? Of course, it's okay. It's—" fantasmagorical, she wanted to shout, "—awfully nice of you."

They unhitched their horses and led them outside. The brilliant contrast to the barn's darkness made Marcy blink. Bert was already in the saddle by the time her eyes had adjusted comfortably. She swung onto the Appaloosa, and they rode out the lane at a brisk walk.

Marcy studied Bert closely and tried to read his mood. She couldn't. She grudgingly concluded she simply didn't know enough about this tall, weathered stranger beside her to read his mood, thoughts, feelings, or anything else. She hated the uneasiness, the nervousness that gripped her when she was in his presence.

She longed to say all the right things, to make all the right moves. She wanted him to know how desperately she had loved him long ago and how desperately she wanted to know him now. But she must never throw herself at him like she did on the beach. So she guarded her thoughts closely, weighed her words carefully, and framed her questions prudently.

"I would have thought Nickle and the guests would have been back from the trail ride by now," Marcy broke the silence.

"Would you rather have made this trip with him?" Bert's face was blank, but his voice was edgy.

74

"Heavens no, Bert!" Marcy answered. Could he possibly be jealous? "Actually, I was thinking of one of the guests. Mr. Percy, the older gentleman from England, referred to the group as tenderfeet. He was a little concerned that the portion of his anatomy that would be the tenderest wouldn't be his feet."

The joke was as old as horses and sore muscles, but Bert grinned and nodded. "I'm afraid Greer overdoes it, sometimes. He forgets that because he could live in the saddle doesn't mean everybody else can. Still, I don't feel I could send Cole on a trip like that. He's such a kid, I'm not sure he'd be mature enough to handle it properly."

"He certainly is full of fun," Marcy agreed. "I think he's cute."

"He's full of, well, foolishness. That boy is serious about two things in his life—chewing tobacco and roping. Everything else is one big joke."

He spoke disparagingly, but Marcy could tell he was fond of the youngster. "The guests get a kick out of him," she said, "and I guess he'll grow out of a lot of that."

"Sure. He's just like a two-year-old colt in training—old enough to know what to do, but too silly to do it. If he sticks around here long enough though, he'll make one heck of a good hand."

His words made Marcy's memory race backward to the barn in suburban Atlanta where the young manager, Bert, was very strict about the type of language she would hear and the type of behavior she would witness.

"But Greer should know better than to keep a bunch of nonriders out for more than three or four hours," he continued. "I'll bet he has nipped some potential horse careers right in the bud on these day-long jaunts."

"Well, boss man, that only leaves one more wrangler who could do it," Marcy teased.

Bert cut his eyes sideways at her and shot his brows up so sharply his hat rocked back. "I'll do that when mustangs ice skate in you-know-where." he vowed.

Marcy laughed. "Well, Nickle is good with your visitors."

"Yeah, I know. He's sort of in charge of public relations, and he's good at it. Truth is, he's a topnotch all-around hand."

They rode a few minutes without speaking, then Marcy ventured a question. "Had you been riding, you and Chief, before I got to the barn?"

"No, why?"

"I was scratching his head and noticed he was sweating under his bridle." She added quickly, "I thought maybe if he'd been out already, I didn't have to—"

"Nobody's been on him. I guess I just saddled up a little early. Besides, it's warm today." As if to underline his observation, he removed his hat and made a swipe across his forehead with the back of his hand.

Marcy noticed a defensive edge to Bert's voice, and took it as a warning to tread softly. "Yes, it is," she agreed. "And thank Heaven for this breeze."

Bert nodded and let his gaze drift idly across

the distant fields, a blanket of restful green, embroidered in the cross-stitch of white fencing. Silence fell again, and Marcy let it be. Their silence wasn't a burdensome one, but her own tension ebbed and flowed in her like a tidal pool.

She was fearful of prying, of invading his privacy, his life, or even his thoughts. Yet she longed to know so much, to ask so many things. The Bert she had loved was warm, open, good-natured, humorous, and tough. The man she rode beside today was distant, guarded, reserved, tight-lipped, and acutely sensitive. Was this the product of maturity and responsibility? Did the ambitious young cowboy sacrifice his fun-loving, affectionate self to become a hard-nosed, withdrawn businessman-rancher? Did he mortgage enjoyment of life to obtain success?

Marcy took in his features in hastily stolen glances. His face bore the thick, weathered mask of an outdoorsman. Yet, in spite of the first hint of crows' feet, the little concave crevices where dimples used to appear, the furrowed brow and deeply lined nick, he didn't look much older than his thirty-one years. He was still thin and hard-muscled, angular, and square-jawed. Nothing had sagged or softened. His virility was not forced or flaunted. It was an aura, an understatement that Marcy found tantalizing.

Something in her would not accept the absolute demise of the Bert she loved, *her* Bert. If this stern and stuffy one belonged to the sterner and stuffier Lisa, then they probably deserved each other. Her Bert had spoken to her, held her, and wept with her on the beach one evening a few days before. And that was the one she watched for and waited to see. The briefest glimpse, the most veiled appearance of him could fan the flames of hope smoldering in her heart.

Marcy knew she mustn't probe for the part of him she loved. At the same time, she wanted him to know she still cared and cared deeply. It was this balancing act on the tightrope between invasion and honest concern that filled her with anxiety.

She began a new conversation. "How far is it to the breeding barns?"

"About a twenty-minute ride," he answered casually. "Most visitors aren't encouraged to make this trip."

"Too many high-priced animals to expose to greenhorns, huh?"

Bert grinned. "It's not so much the price of the stock, though we wouldn't want them accidentally turned loose or sneaked out of the barn for a joyride. My main concern is the risk. We have a barn full of stallions, ours and other peoples'. Some of them are big pets, and Great Aunt Jane would be welcome to reach in and pat them on the nose. Some of them aren't. If Great Aunt Jane were lucky, she might just be missing a few fingers. If she weren't lucky, one might crash right through the wall after her."

Marcy shuddered, as a mingling of awe, fright and admiration coursed through her. She knew a high-strung, enraged, or enamored stallion is one of the most fearsome creatures on earth; also one of the most magnificent.

"I have an idea the people who don't get to see them are really missing something."

Bert turned in his saddle to face her and confessed, "I'm awfully proud of them."

For a heartbeat the guard was dropped. He spoke from deep within and was sharing a true horseman's pride with one he knew would understand. Marcy smiled, her eyes filled with love. *And I'm awfully proud of you,* she thought.

A couple of cowboys passed them in the lane, spoke to Bert, and touched their hat brims to Marcy. They rode on a few yards, when Bert pulled up sharply. "Wait here a minute, Marcy, I'll be right back." The Pinto wheeled and caught up with the other riders in five or six easy strides.

The Chief fidgeted at the sudden departure of his companion. "Whoa, buddy." Marcy tugged the reins lightly and turned him around so he could see the other horses. Bert conferred briefly with the other two, then jogged back to where she waited.

"Sorry," he apologized, "but I hadn't talked to anybody over here since this morning. An owner was supposed to pick up her mare today, and I wondered if she had." He seemed mildly irritated at whatever he had been told, so Marcy kept quiet.

When they resumed their journey, she noticed two gleaming metal roofs, quivering beneath rising heat waves. As they neared the barns, she was able to see which was the mares' barn and which was the studs'. The mares milled peacefully and grazed in a large, fenced paddock that covered several acres. Across a gravel lot the stallions' barn was surrounded by long, sturdy rectangles or "runs" built of tubular steel, to keep them separated. Nature had decreed in ages past that the males were not as willing to live together in harmony as females.

The barns were plain, but neat and spotlessly white-washed. "Good-looking barns," Marcy observed, more to herself than to Bert.

"Thanks," he answered, vacantly.

Though determined to take this man beside her as he was, Marcy couldn't help wondering why he seemed so preoccupied in her presence. What was it that bled his concentration from her? Except for their first few minutes together on the beach, she felt as if every meeting was conducted with Bert's attention at a full gallop in every direction but toward her. His politeness was an empty courtesy, not friendliness.

When she saw they were going to be alone together on this excursion, she had dared to hope she would at least fill his awareness, if not his memory. And perhaps she had, in isolated instances. Still, he waited just outside a fortress of defensiveness, poised to dash behind its protective walls at the slightest threat. Whatever the two cowhands on the road told him had dissolved Marcy's prospects for a friendly get-acquainted or re-acquainted afternoon. His expression of vague annoyance had settled into a deepening scowl.

They dismounted at the mare barn and looped one rein around a convenient hitching rail. Several teen-age boys and girls with wheelbarrows and shovels were mucking-out the stalls. One fresh-faced redhead in pigtails called, "Hi, Mr. Treece," but didn't seem to expect an answer.

They stepped into the long, straight hall, and Bert turned toward a door marked, "Office."

"Start on down the hallway," he gestured, "and I'll be back out by the time you get to our number one lady. I've got some things to check on in here."

Checking on things is just about all you do, Marcy thought with a twinge of irritation. But immediately, she realized that was selfish of her. The enormity of Bert's responsibilities was just beginning to become clear to her. The cattle operation, the horse business, the tourist program, and management of all the personnel necessary to keep the Coquina running smoothly were each monumental tasks within themselves. Overseeing them all had to be an extremely demanding schedule of checking on things. Maybe his having so much to do accounts for his remoteness, Marcy conceded, reviving the possibility that she was not the sole source of his moodiness.

The first two stalls she looked into were empty. The third housed an aged white mare, dozing with her head in the corner. Her name and a short pedigree hung on her door. Marcy didn't recognize her bloodlines and decided not to rouse her.

Next was a two-year-old filly, according to her identification sign. She was almost jet black with a light sprinkling of snow across her hips. She was wide-eyed and curious, but Marcy couldn't coax her closer than the center of her stall.

Bays, sorrels, whites, leopards, and one palomino greeted their visitor with varying degrees of receptiveness. Some of the youngsters were cautious and shy. Others were boldly friendly. Most of the older mares appeared imperturbable, accepting or rejecting Marcy's attentions with a calm serenity born of the wisdom and maturity of years of motherhood.

Marcy was fascinated by the Appaloosa's coat patterns. The classic markings involved one solid color with a white blanket over the hips. Spots of the main color or a completely different color usually appeared in the blanket. But it was the endless variations of patterns that made the breed unique. The blanket sometimes drifted along the back toward the shoulders. Often, the spots are encircled with "smoke rings," lighter bands of the spot color. The leopard Appaloosas were spotted all over, with the size of the circles usually growing as they neared the hips. Then there were the roans, red, gray, or blue-black, with markings as varied and individual as human fingerprints.

Marcy was three-quarters of the way through the barn, when Bert joined her. "How do you like our girls?" he asked.

"They're simply gorgeous, Bert. Are they all Coquina mares?"

"The ones with nameplates on the doors are. The unidentified ones are outside mares here for breeding. Our pride and joy is here in this next stall." He opened the door and stepped inside. Marcy followed.

A buckskin mare with a black mane and tail and black spots in a white blanket approached them placidly, as if admiration and stroking were part of her everyday life. Marcy ran her hand along the silken neck and back. "Oh, you beautiful animal. Bert, I have never seen this color combination."

"Neither had anybody around here, until she came along. She was born on the ranch a little before my time. They tell me her dam was sort of a muddy palomino with white spots, and her sire was dark bay with a solid blanket. She has given us some loud-colored babies, but none of them have repeated her colors. You'll see one of her colts in the stud barn."

Marcy could hardly tear her eyes away from the flashy horse, but she knew they needed to move along. As Bert closed the stall door, she read her name, "Coquina's Bonny B."

"She's a straight line descendant from Joker B."

"No wonder she's special," Marcy observed.

"Shall we go see the boys?" Bert's tone was almost jovial.

"By all means."

Squinting against the brilliant sunlight, they started across the lot toward the second barn. Marcy noticed a maroon pick-up truck with a matching two-horse trailer behind it, parked in an area with some other vehicles. The writing on the trailer was obscured until they passed alongside. "Lisa Calloway, Quarter Horses, Sarasota, Florida" leaped out at her in blazing white letters.

Her again, was the first impression Marcy was able to sort out. Was that woman to loom like a ghost over everything she did, everywhere she went throughout her entire vacation? Even her truck and trailer were shiny and spotless. Perfect, just like Lisa.

For some reason, she felt a little relieved to discover Lisa lived a fair distance from the Coquina. Some connection with Bert was undeniable, that she was more than an ordinary guest was obvious, but at least, she wasn't a permanent fixture on the ranch. Whatever the outcome, Marcy decided to risk a question or two.

"I see Miss Calloway is from Sarasota."

Bert looked puzzled, then glanced at the trailer. "Yeah. She owns a travel agency there."

"Does she have some good quarter horses?"

"Okay, I guess. She brought a nice mare to one of our stallions."

"Oh? Did we see her in the barn?"

"No, she's out on pasture."

"Do you get a lot of owners who stay on as guests while their mares are here?"

"No."

Marcy was out of innocent questions. Anything else she asked would be obvious and revealing. Bert had relaxed visibly while showing her Bonny B., but tension was again tightening his features. *Is it me?* Marcy thought. *Is it Lisa? Is it both of us here at the same time?* She seriously doubted that the latter was the case. *I certainly haven't been around Bert enough to cramp his style. In fact, he doesn't seem to care much that I'm here at all.*

They entered the second barn, and Bert made straight for a stall midway down the hall. Shoving open the door, he said, "this is our number one man, Applaud Me. He's a Prince Plaudit horse."

84

Marcy held out her hand tentatively and watched his ears closely. She was prepared to withdraw at the first sign of ill temper. But the white and brown face held big, warm eyes, and he offered nothing but friendship. "Ooh, he's gorgeous, too. He looks like somebody flipped spoonfuls of cocoa powder on him."

Bert was standing at his shoulder, rubbing his neck. He wasn't smiling, but Marcy saw a light in his eyes she had seen many times before. It was a radiation of admiration, pride, and genuine affection for the species, as well as the stallion. It was a glow Marcy often felt herself when looking at truly superior stock. She wondered if it showed in her as clearly as it did in Bert.

"Hi, boy," she spoke softly, as she petted his face and nose. "How old is he?"

"He's five. He does real well in halter classes. We haven't shown him in much else."

"Do you show him, yourself?"

"I do when I can get away from here. Which isn't as much as I'd like to, sometimes, but I'm not complaining. Greer does a good job, when I can't go."

They closed the door on the reigning king of the Coquina Ranch and strolled on down the hall. "Do you still break and train horses?" Marcy asked, recalled what well-mannered mounts he used to produce.

"Some. I'm working on him," he indicated the horse they had just left. "I've gotten several colts started, but I'm only able to finish out one or two a year. I have so much else to do. But you know me, I'd a lot rather be out here in these barns than corralled in an office."

His last words sent a surge of delight through Marcy. She wanted to jump up and down and shout, *Yes, yes! I do know you! Thanks for remembering!* "I'll bet you would," she said. "By the way, with all these Apps around here why do you still ride a pinto?"

"I guess you could say I'm devoted to Appaloosas, but my favorite horse, purely and simply, is a pinto. Always had been, probably always will be."

"Whatever happened to Jimbo?" she continued and knew immediately she had made a mistake.

He recoiled visibly. "He fell in a trailer on the way to a show and broke his neck." Before Marcy could voice her sympathy, he went on, "If you'll excuse me, again, I need to step into this office, too, for a minute. Go on and look around, but be careful. We have some savage biters in here."

"Sure, go ahead. I'll just look and not touch. Where is Bonny B.'s colt you said was over here?"

"He's on the other side of the hall, down at the far end." He pointed toward the door they had come in.

Marcy fought anger at herself for asking unfortunate questions and at Bert for being so sensitive or delicate or whatever he was. *I'm so tired of this elevator I'm on around him*, she thought. *Up, down, up, down, and it doesn't take anything to push the wrong button.*

She reached the door marked Bonny B.'s Bear Paw. As she looked in at the young horse, all her anger, self-pity and anguish over Bert dissolved in an icy rush of fear. The colt stood in the middle of his stall, his back hunched deeply. He turned a puzzled, miserable gaze on Marcy, then resumed staring at the wall in front of him. "Oh, no," she breathed.

Almost without realizing what she was doing, she opened the door and stepped into his stall. He aimed another short, worried look at her, but made no effort to move. She approached him slowly and quietly. "Easy, little fellow. It's all right," she cooed. He was motionless as she ran her hand down the taut muscles of his charcoal gray back and across his white-blanketed hips. His flanks were trembling slightly, and his hair was beginning to dampen.

She backed out of the stall, slammed the door and ran toward to office. "Bert!" she shrieked, still running. "Bert! Hurry!"

The office door flew open and banged against the wall. A young man stood in the doorway, obviously wondering about the commotion. Bert caught Marcy by the shoulders. "What it it? What's wrong?"

Marcy was panting. "It's Bear Paw. He looks like he has colic."

They all three burst down the hall, then Bert halted and turned to the young man. "Get on the phone and get Greer over here, *now*." Then to himself, "Boy, he'd better be back from that trail ride."

Marcy had to run to keep up with Bert. When they reached his stall, Bear Paw was standing much as Marcy had left him, but he was pawing delicately with one forefoot.

"Oh, no, you don't, Squirt," Bert ordered, as he threw open the door and leaped inside. "You're going to stay up on all four of those little feet." He put one arm around the colt's neck and rested the other hand on his nose.

"Can I do anything?" Marcy offered.

"Yeah, go back to the office and get his halter and a lead rope."

She went quickly and when she returned, Bert was walking Bear Paw around in circles with a makeshift halter. He slipped the leather halter on and led him out into the hallway. The little horse followed reluctantly.

"Do you think he's been like this long?" Marcy was worried.

"No, he's just now beginning to sweat. But it's a good thing you caught it. I was going to go out the other door and get our horses. I wouldn't have seen him."

Bert led the colt outside, untied his own horse and stepped up on him, just as the foreman arrived in the Bronco. Nickle eyed Bear Paw sharply. "Is it bad?"

"I don't think so, yet, and with a little luck, we'll get to work on it before it gets much worse. You get everything ready. The Old Man and I are going to take the baby for a walk." Bert looped the lead rope once around his saddle horn and urged his horse into a walk. Bear Paw, woebegone and pathetic, plodded listlessly along behind the big pinto. As they moved away from her, Marcy noticed a brown spot in his blanket slightly to the left and above his tail. It was shaped exactly like a black ink imprint of a bear's foot, apparently the reason for his name.

"Bless his little heart," Marcy felt her eyes burning. She looked up at Nickle. "What are you going to do for him?"

"We'll try to get his plumbing working again. The main thing will be to keep him moving and not let him lie down and roll. He might twist an intestine, and that would be the end of Bear Paw. If we don't break it soon, Dr. Rinehart will take over. Look, I hate to rush off, but I'd better get busy."

"Go ahead. I'm going to start back. Let me know how he is."

The Chief stood alone at the hitching post, dozing in the late afternoon sun. "It's just the two of us, boy," she said, as she climbed into the saddle, then added, "again."

The waning day was cooling noticeably. Because all her attention had been claimed on the trip over by her companion, Marcy was now more aware of her surroundings. She was grateful for the opportunity to retrace her steps through the beautiful ranch land. She couldn't help worrying about the colt, nor could she keep herself from rehashing the realities and nuances of the enigma named Tolbert Treece.

Even so, she was able to appreciate the sparkling green fields, shimmering now through the mist of lazily rotating irrigation sprays. Adam's Flannel, with its soft, feltlike leaves and its crowning spikes of yellow flowers, spring up here and there along the road, like torches lighting the way. Occasionally, even in the plush, well-groomed pastures, the saffron blossoms rose five feet from the earth in lofty triumph.

The "sweet-sweet" of an unseen sandpiper floated barely into earshot on a passing breeze and reminded Marcy of the beach. Day's end was her favorite time to stroll at the water's edge or swim. But she had no desire to hurry back, and she promised herself a sunset visit to the ocean tomorrow. Tonight, dusk would find her alone with a nice, quiet, accommodating friend, possibly the best friend she had, at the moment. She petted Chief Joseph on the neck. "You're such a sweetheart," she told him.

She used a few of those moments bathed in the splendor of the Creator's handiwork to pray. "Thank You, Father, for this wonderful animal and this beautiful place. Forgive me for what I'm doing wrong and for what I can't let go and let You handle. And, Lord, touch little Bear Paw with the hand of the greatest physician the world has ever known. He is Yours, intricately and beautifully created."

She wrestled with her mind in an effort to keep it off Bert. She was tired of the seering doubts that lapped at her like tiny, unextinguishable flames after every encounter with him. She was tired of wondering why he had said what he said, or why he didn't say something. She was tired of wondering why he reacted as he did to some of the things she said. It was all so exasperating, she would rather not bother with thinking about him at all. But, bother she would, probably for a long, long time.

Had Bert taken her to the breeding barns in response to her request that they be friends? Had he saddled up early out of anticipation, or eagerness to be done with it. Did he enjoy being with her, or dread it?

The fiery western glow was dying as Marcy left the barn and walked toward the dining room. Chief was unsaddled, curried, and grinding away at his evening meal. She picked up a ham sandwich and a salad to eat in her room.

After supper, she switched on the television and stretched out one her bed to watch it. Sometime during the first hour of the Movie of the Week, she dropped off to sleep. Jolted awake by an unidentifiable noise, she sat up and looked at her watch. Ten-thirty. An insistent banging on her door made her jump. "Who it it?"

It was a man's voice, but his muffled answer was unintelligible, so she moved to the door and asked, "Nickle? Is that you?"

"No," her caller replied. "It's Bert."

CHAPTER 6

BERT? Marcy opened the door in a fog of sleep and amazement.

"Sorry, if you were expecting Greer," he said.

"No, I wasn't. Come in." Marcy stepped back. "I was just hoping for—"

Bert cut her off. "I won't come in. It's too late to intrude. At least you weren't in bed, yet. I stopped by to tell you the colt is all right. I thought you might want to know."

"Oh, thank God! I'm so glad. And Bert, you're not intruding. I had just fallen asleep watching—"

"I've got to get back," he interrupted again. He replaced his hat, which he had been holding, and stepped off the porch. "Good night."

All of the tensions of Marcy's afternoon came to a rapid boil, heated a few extra degrees by the sudden awakening. Her system's defenses were low, and her control was less than adequate.

She stepped in the doorway and shouted after the retreating figure, "Stop interrupting me and listen! I was not expecting Nickle! I was hoping for some word on Bear Paw, and I knew if anyone would think to tell me, he would. I never expected," she cried furiously into the darkness, "you to care about whether I was worried or not!"

Marcy was fighting tears when she slammed her door. "As if it mattered anyway!" she hissed, ripping her covers back and sending her pillow ricocheting off the wall. Her hands trembled, as she undressed and prepared for bed. She was as angry at his ability to upset her as she was at his attitude. It was that anger—at her trembling hands and watery eyes—she turned upon herself.

She slid between the sheets, not relaxed enough for sleep, but calmer.

Had he come to her bunkhouse simply to inform her of Bear Paw's recovery? Had her assumption that it was the foreman at the door bruised a frail ego or stirred actual feelings of jealousy? Marcy recalled a similar reaction earlier. Could he possibly have witnessed Nickle's intended kiss? Yet, if he cared enough to be jealous, why had he practically denied her presence here?

She fell into a troubled sleep.

Marcy rose early and was at poolside by nine o'clock. She sunbathed as long as she dared and spent the afternoon reading in the shade and chatting with other guests. As she had promised herself, she dressed for riding and went to the barn shortly before sundown.

Nickle was finishing up his chores and greeted her warmly. "Come to take the Chief for an evening jaunt?"

"Yes, if I may," she answered. "Is he finished eating?"

At the sound of her voice, the Appaloosa nickered.

"Well, well, well," the foreman looked surprised. "Looks like you two have become chummy. I think he just asked you where you've been all day."

Marcy went to his stall and patted his head through the slats. "I've missed you too, boy." She noticed his grain box was not quite empty, so she turned back to Nickle. "Was Bear Paw still well this morning?"

"Yeah, that little scoundrel seems fit as a fiddle. The boss man stayed with him all night, just to play it safe."

"I'm so glad he's okay."

"The boss man has put together quite an operation over there, hasn't he? Did you enjoy your tour?"

If Marcy hadn't been looking at Nickle, she would not have detected the subtle change in his expression to an apprehensive, guarded look.

She paused only a moment. "Yes, he has some magnificent horses. It's quite a set-up. I don't see how he does it all."

"The boss man is nothing if not efficient," he said. "He does have a lot to do, but he could lighten the load if he would delegate authority a little more. As it is, we all have our jobs, and he has his and ours, too. You have to hand it to him, though. He has doubled the breeding program, upgraded the Santa Gertrudis herd, and hung onto the tourist business."

"It's easy to see where his heart lies," Marcy observed. *What is it between those two?* she reflected. The relationship seemed to be one of strained admiration, grudging respect. She had noticed the same thing from Bert, but the first person he had sought in the crisis with Bear Paw was Nickle.

"I guess you did a lot of catching up on old times, huh?" he said with hesitation.

Marcy wasn't sure how to answer him. There was only one truthful answer of course, but she felt it was necessary to give herself away. Yet, she didn't want to hurt Nickle's feelings by sounding chummy with his boss, either. "Not really," she hedged.

Nickle looked up from the bridle he was cleaning. His eyes made a mute appeal, for what, Marcy wasn't sure. "The truth is, Nickle," she admitted, "Old times didn't come up at all."

The foreman's attention returned to his task. "That's too bad," his tone was noncommittal. "I'll have to admit," he added slowly, "I was counting on taking you over there, myself." This time he didn't look up.

"I'd love to go back," Marcy hastily assured him. "Except for a little time spent with Bonny B., Applaud Me and, unfortunately, Bear Paw, I was pretty much on my own. Bert had to check in at both offices."

"See?" His good humor was apparently restored. "If I had taken you, I could've told you all about everybody's mama and daddy and grandmama and granddaddy." He disappeared into the tack room and returned with Chief's blanket, saddle and bridle.

Marcy checked Chief's feed box, found it empty this time and led him out to where Nickle waited with his gear.

In a few moments Chief's tack was in place. "There you go," Nickle said, making one last tug at the cinch strap.

Marcy led the horse outside, and Nickle followed. As she put her foot into the stirrup, he inquired hesitantly, "Want some company?"

"Sure." Marcy didn't sound convincing to her own ears.

"Great! Let me get my . . ." His last word was drowned out by the shrill insistence of a telephone bell. He grimaced, shrugged and went into the office. In less than a minute, he was back, looking clearly disappointed. "Sorry," he said, "Maybe some other time. That was the boss man saying he had to leave, and he's expecting some hifalootin' mare up from Miami. He wants me to go over to the barn and wait for her."

"That's okay. We'll go for a ride real soon," she promised. "And Nickle, thank you." Nickle had been so nice to her, and she would have found him an enjoyable riding companion, but she was a little relieved he wouldn't be making this particular trip. She hadn't forgotten his closeness by the hay wagon that night and she felt a little torn about her feelings toward him. She needed more time to sort things out.

Marcy rode to where the beach began. She dismounted and slipped off her boots, murmuring to Chief, "There's something about warm, soft sand." Only a few days ago, she had made this same ride, pulled off these same boots and walked smack into her greatest emotional upheaval since her childhood separation from Bert.

She propped her boots against the rough, spiny wood of a coco palm. Her eyes traveled up its trunk and came to rest in its umbrella of foliage, all the greener for its clear azure backdrop.

The beach was alive with all that Marcy loved about the seashore. Gulls argued loudly in their strident, shrieking way. A large brown pelican rested on a ragged projection that had once been a wall. About the time she decided he was asleep, he took to the air with a grace always unexpected from such an ungainly appearance. He circled slowly a few times, made an arrowhead of himself and plunged cleanly into the water, barely disturbing its surface. He emerged with a glittering silver fish crosswise in his beak. With an almost imperceptible snap of his neck, the glimmering catch disappeared, and he bobbed contentedly on the water. The distractions were all welcome to her, and she was able to appreciate the glories of creation unhindered by her worries.

Marcy watched the magnificent kaleidoscope of color with awe and heart-felt appreciation for the beauty God chose to weave into His creation. Scarlet clouds deepening into purple with the final rays of the vanishing day. Night would come, another soft, velvety one. The grandeur of nature never failed to move her. Her Appaloosa escort was silent and practically motionless whenever she stopped. She wondered if, somehow, in a way unknown to human consciousness, animals could perceive the glories of the world around them. She wanted to believe they could. She was sure Chief Joseph felt her admiration and growing love for him, because of the way he responded to her.

"You are the most fantastic horse," she declared, looking up into one warm, brown eye. The spell was broken, and he nuzzled her ear playfully. "We'd better start back, or somebody will send out a search party."

Marcy rounded the turn into the barn and saw that the office lights were on. She slid the saddle off and was just starting to remove the bridle when Bert stepped through the office door.

"I noticed the Chief was gone, and assumed you had him. I've been waiting for you," he added.

"Oh?" Marcy didn't want to seem coy, but she refused to feel guilty for being late to a meeting she never dreamed awaited her.

His tone softened. "I wanted to apologize for last night. I'm sorry I snapped your head off. Your life, especially while you are here, is none of my business."

"Did you hear what I said to you as you left?"

"Yes. That's what made me realize how out of line I was."

"Don't worry about it," Marcy tried to be comforting and matter-of-fact at the same time.

"You'd had a bad afternoon and were facing a long night."

"That's no excuse. It was a cut and dried case of ill manners and bad behavior, and I feel terrible about it. Marcy, what you do with Greer or anybody else *can't* matter to me." He emphasized "can't" with a note of supplication that was reflected in his face. It was as if he were begging her to understand something he was unable to explain.

"Well," she said, "don't worry about it. Nickle has been a friend to me here."

"By the way," she said, breaking from her reverie, "you certainly look snazzy."

Her eyes swept him from head to toe. He wore a deep green western suit, white shirt, and a green stockman's tie. His boots and hat were both gray-green. *Mercy, he's handsome,* she repeated to herself like a stuck record. "Green certainly is your color."

"Thanks," he shoved his hands into his pockets and looked away. "I hope that is the last time I'll have to follow up a conversation with an apology. It's getting to be a habit."

Before Marcy could reply, a steel blue Mercedes glided into the barn lot. Its driver blew the horn in sharp, staccato blasts.

"I believe we have some impatient company," Marcy remarked.

"That's my car. I'm late for a . . . an appointment." He tipped his hat and strode toward the car.

Marcy thought he looked dispirited and tired, as he climbed behind the wheel. She couldn't make out the other person in the car until the window lowered and a voice purred, "Good night, Miss DeLaney."

Lisa! She should have known.

She no longer felt any doubt that Bert and Lisa were "seeing each other socially," as they say. And that discovery was actually more a relief than anything else. The prospect of Bert's spending an evening with Lisa Calloway evoked feelings of pity rather than envy; he didn't seem to enjoy her company. Since she no longer wondered *if* they were a pair, she now wondered *why*.

"You've been very patient," she said to the horse. "I guess you'd like for me to finish with you."

She slipped his bridle off and his halter on and snapped the lead onto a cross-tie ring. She brushed him and turned him in his stall. She was going into the feed room when Nickle's voice startled her.

"Hey! He's been fed, remember?" he shouted from the far end of the hall.

"I remember," she called, and proceeded to the feed room. She came out with grain in her cupped hand and met him at the horse's stall. "I think he deserves a treat for being such a good boy. I don't have much."

Nickle smiled and shook his head. "You wouldn't spoil a fellow's horse, would you?"

"Me? Heavens no!"

"Have a good ride?"

"Yes, it was beautiful. Did your Miami mare get here?"

"Yep, she's all squared away. And before you ask, yes, Bear Paw is still fine."

"That's great!"

"The boss man sure credits you with finding him in time. Have you seen much colic in horses?"

"No, not much. But I've seen it enough to remember it. My diagnosis was based on a lot of fear and a little experience."

They then stood in several minutes of awkward silence. She felt Nickle wanted to pose questions he couldn't phrase, and she wanted to ask him about Bert. She spoke first testing the water with a general observation. "Your boss certainly did look tired tonight."

"You'd probably look tired too if you'd spent the night with a young horse," he answered tartly.

The surprise was so evident on Marcy's face, he spoke again quickly. "I'm sorry, Marcy. I didn't mean that the way it sounded. I guess Her Majesty, Miz-z-z Calloway, has all of us a little on edge."

"So I've noticed," Marcy said. "Can't anyone tell me why?"

Nickle looked at her thoughtfully, as if arguing with himself about what to say next. He finally spoke quietly, with just a hint of sorrow. "Yes, someone can. But it will have to be when he's ready. It's not my place to discuss a personal situation I know very little about. And the other hands know less than I do. I can tell you he hasn't been the same man since she came back, and he has been even less himself since you showed up. Both of you being here at the same time has been a hard ride.''

"What has he told you about us?" Marcy was taken off guard by Nickle's frankness.

"Nothing. He didn't have to. You've told me all I've needed to know to understand why the boss man's in such a tailspin.''

Fully aware that she had never discussed her and Bert's relationship with Nickle, Marcy blushed hotly. She thought the few times she had tried to get information from him, she had done so without giving herself away. She asked timidly, "Am I that transparent?"

Nickle's gaze was fixed somewhere beyond her down the barn hall. He might have been looking at a nail head, a horse, or the farthest constellation, his eyes were so vacant.

"Only to someone who could care more than he should.''

CHAPTER 7

MARCY COULD NOT HAVE BEEN MORE STUNNED if someone had burst a water-filled balloon over her head.

"Good night," Nickle turned hastily and left the barn. Then, over his shoulder, he called, "You know where the lights are."

"Well!" she said aloud, standing alone in the hall. "How much more complicated are things going to get?"

She turned off the barn lights and walked slowly toward Bunkhouse Number Three, musing on what the evening had revealed to her. She had learned that Bert was upset because Lisa was there, but he was more upset because she was there, too. And she had learned that Bert had something to tell her, and he was finding it hard to do.

That bit of knowledge gave her a sinking feeling. If it was so hard to tell her, it must be bad. The only glimmer of encouragement was the possibility that he felt discomfort because he still cared for her. Even that could be her imagination.

After sifting through the facts, if she could call them facts, concerning Bert and Lisa, she came again to Nickle. How foolish, no, stupid of her, she scolded herself, for not seeing that Nickle's interest went deeper than she had realized. Thinking back, she had gotten her first clue the day she arrived. The way he looked at her while she stood on the fence petting the Chief. What about that night after the barbecue, when he walked her to her cabin after Lisa's verbal attack? That exchange was more than casual, and she had known it at the time. And there was the trip to the breeding barns and those rides he tried to arrange with her. She never deliberately toyed with anyone's feelings. Had she been heartless toward Nickle? Or, had she been so completely wrapped in the cocoon of Bert that she saw and felt Nickle's attraction to her—and her own to him—but it simply hadn't registered?

She liked Nickle. She would hate to see him hurt over anyone, particularly her. For a fraction of a moment, she thought of Nickle in a different light. Things looked pretty bleak for her and Bert. Nickle was good-looking, friendly, and fun. He had an easy, comfortable spiritual confidence that she found attractive in a man. But honesty asserted itself, and she was forced to admit—again—that anyone besides Bert would be a substitute. Nickle was a friend and deserved more than that.

As Marcy passed the arena, she heard young Jesse Cole talking to several other cowboys. She had no intention of listening to their conversation until she heard the name Lisa. Noiselessly, she moved closer to the group of boys, keeping in the deepest shadows.

"Yeah, that's her mare," said a voice Marcy didn't recognize.

The next words were muffled, but they got a unanimous if somewhat subdued agreement from the listeners.

"He's been like that ever since his old lady moved in on him again." That contribution was Jesse's.

Old lady? Moved in? Could Lisa be Bert's *wife?*

Marcy stumbled blindly, fighting her way through tears and underbrush back to the path. She scraped her shoulder on an unseen tree or post, and a sharp yucca spine pricked her thigh.

In her desperation to not hear another word, Marcy had to fight the impulse to run with her hands clasped firmly over her ears. Her tears were flowing freely, and she pretended that her injuries were the reason.

By the time she reached her bunkhouse door, her disappointment and surprise were melting into anger. "Why couldn't he have told me that?" she demanded of no one, as she burst into her room. "How hard can it be to say, 'Oh, by the way, Marcy, I'm married'?"

Her mind ran the all too familiar obstacle course of questions—one it had run more in the last week than in all the past seven years put together: Why hadn't Nickle told her when she asked him who Lisa was?

She made a quick examination of her wounds and diagnosed them as superficial. She sat on the edge of her bed, arranging her thoughts and subduing her feelings. If they were married, why did she have her own business in Sarasota? If they were separated, why did they see each other so often? Was she absolutely sure, beyond a reasonable doubt, that Tolbert Treece and Lisa Calloway were married to each other?

No.

But they could be. She might have developed her business before they were married, and she refused to give it up. That would also account for the continued use of her maiden name. That would fit in, too, with Nickle's scornful emphasis on the prefix 'Ms.' before her name.

Their being married would explain so many things. Bert's preoccupation and defensiveness. His nervousness in her presence. He probably wondered if she would catch them talking.

It would also explain Lisa's instant dislike of her. Bert had obviously told her something about them, but how much and with what approach, Marcy didn't know. Old chums of days gone by? Past acquaintances? Childhood sweethearts? It wasn't likely that Lisa would feel animosity toward someone who had been described as an unimportant, obscure figure from her husband's past.

The next few days were calm and uneventful, and Marcy was grateful. She did not cross paths with Bert, Lisa or the foreman. Her hours were spent riding Chief Joseph, sunbathing by the pool with her fellow vacationers, or strolling along the beach.

The barn was usually empty when she saddled up the Appaloosa and when she brought him back. Occasionally, there were a couple of working ranch hands she hadn't met, but a simple greeting or nod was all they expected. She presumed preparations for the upcoming rodeo claimed most of Nickle's time. She hoped he wasn't avoiding her out of embarrassment.

She thought about Bert as little as possible. Imagining where he was or what he was doing confused and distressed her, so she tried to avoid it.

During the day she let sunshine and sea breezes fill her heart, mind and soul. One afternoon, she rode double with young Eric Winfield to the beach on the Chief. It was a genuine pleasure to watch him exult over the colorful shells, gleefully outrun pursuing waves and build, with great planning and concentration, a subdivision in the sand.

Eric threw himself into his hours by the water with the total commitment of childhood. *Where along the way do we lose our ability to give ourselves over to complete enjoyment in where we are and what we are doing?* she wondered. She saw the little girl Marcy playing in the surf and exploring the beach content and fulfilled.

On a Tuesday morning, Marcy left for the barn after breakfast. She decided to expend her restlessness on Chief Joseph. She wasn't sure where they would go, but maybe they would ride the swamp trail again. Or, maybe they would ride over to the breeding barns again and look in on Little Bear Paw. Wherever she ultimately pointed the horse's nose, she was looking forward to a day in the saddle.

As she neared the barn, she saw Nickle riding toward her on his little buckskin. "Who-o-oa, Buck." He pulled the gelding to a sliding stop in front of her. "Morning, Miss DeLaney." He tipped his hat.

Marcy was instantly reassured by his brilliant smile and answered, "Morning, Mr. Greer." Was he his old self again?

"May I ask where you are bound on this grand and glorious A. M.?"

"You may, but the truth is I don't know. I was going to get the Chief, but where we'll go after I get him, I haven't decided yet."

"Let me guess. The wealthy young traveler is tired of the luxury of leisure, weary of idleness. Right?"

"Mostly. Only make that 'the unemployed young traveler.'"

"As your friendly, neighborhood fun and games coordinator, may I make a suggestion?"

"You may."

He dropped his cavalier's demeanor. "How would you like a funfilled Florida day of manual labor? We're bringing in a bunch of calves and steers for the rodeo, and we need every cowboy—oops, 'scuse me—cowperson we can get."

"Sounds like fun, but I don't know anything about herding cows."

108

"Oh, it'll be fun all right, for about the first hour. The rest of the day might be another story. If you're willing to give it a try, it doesn't matter how much you know about working cattle. Just hang on tight, and Chief Joe will teach you all you need to know."

Marcy had a few qualms, but the prospect of adventure overcame them. "Sure. I'd love it."

"Hold on a minute," he warned. "You'd better just agree to 'try it.' You don't really know yet if you'll love it.'"

"Okay, then, I'll try it. Where do I go after I saddle up?"

"I'm going now to get Cole. I'll come back by here for you."

"I'll hurry," she promised, and ran the rest of the way to the barn. Apparently the Chief absorbed Marcy's excitement. He was impatient while she brushed him, and he danced around when she threw the blanket and saddle onto his back. She was amused at that uncharacteristic behavior, but it only served to heighten her own anticipation.

Riding on an actual round-up was one of the distant fantasies Marcy had entertained. Always, just on the outskirts of the realities of her horse world, she wondered what it would be like to work cattle on a horse. Of course, this wasn't a real round-up, but she would be working cattle. She was both nervous and delighted. What if she fell off? What if she was more in the way than helpful?

The foreman's arrival made her give voice to the last doubt. "Nickle, promise me something, okay?"

"What's that?"

"If I prove to be more of a hindrance than a help, you'll tell me. I realize this isn't tourist entertainment. I don't want to be in the way."

"Don't worry. If you get in the way, you won't have to be told. You'll probably get run over."

"Oh, great! You're so encouraging." She was in the saddle, and they were walking toward the breeding barns.

They were soon joined by Jesse Cole and two other young men. Marcy wondered briefly if they had been in the group the night she overheard them talking about Lisa.

The introductions were cryptic, "Marcy, this is Leo and Dutch."

Marcy said, "Hi."

She had no idea which was Leo and which was Dutch.

Both cowboys said, "Nice ta meetcha."

Jesse gave her as big a smile as he was able with his chipmunk cheeks.

A larger group of mounted riders congregated in the road ahead. As they drew closer, Marcy was relieved to see two other females in the bunch, then she hoped fervently the three of them weren't along to cook for the ranch hands.

Again, Nickle made short introductions. "Folks, this is Marcy. There are Jim, Charlie, Bad Eye, Sue, Freddie, Horse Man, and Casey. Let's go, everybody."

Nickle trotted up to the head of the riders, and Marcy felt suddenly abandoned. Her nervousness retured, as she surveyed the assembly of seasoned ranch hands.

She tried to put names with faces, but if the owner hadn't made some small gesture at his or her name, she didn't know which ones went with whom. She was pretty sure the one Nickle called Horse Man was an Indian. When the name Freddie was called, a dusty teenager had made a peace sign at her. And Bad Eye just about had to be the only one wearing glasses.

As Marcy was pondering the people about her, a young lady with pigtails pulled out of a small knot of riders and fell in beside her. She remembered having seen her at the breeding barns. "Hi, I'm Casey McKee," she said, with an easy, natural friendliness. "If you caught who everybody is, it's a miracle."

"Hi, Casey," Marcy laughed. "I've been trying to decide who's who, but I'm not getting very far."

Casey went through the names, pointed out the appropriate individuals, and offered an item or two of interest. "Charlie and Bad Eye are brothers, Sue is Charlie's wife. Jim has been on the ranch forever, and Freddie only came here this summer.

"Horse Man is a ghost who only appears to us during rodeo time," she confided in a low voice.

"Thank the Great Spirit he does," came from somewhere in the middle of the group, "or else I don't see how you would ever manage." When he turned and looked unsmiling at them, Marcy realized it was the Indian doing the talking. Just when she was about to take his sternness seriously, he winked.

Marcy returned her attention to Casey.

"Thanks. Now I know who they are, if I can only remember."

"This your first cattle work?" Casey asked.

Marcy nodded slowly and felt her brow knit with misgivings.

Casey grinned. "Come here and let me give you a tip."

Marcy eased the Chief close to Casey's bay Appaloosa mare.

"Tie a knot in your reins right about here." Casey dropped her own reins and tied Marcy's together just above the spot where she held them. "Then tie another here, close to the end. When the action starts, bring the ends of your reins up through the hole under the pommel and hook this second knot over the horn. Then you won't have to worry about the reins, and they'll still be where you can get to them. Pay close attention to Chief's head and ears and which calf he's after. About all you'll have to do is hang on. When the calf is where you want him, or you want to rein Chief off of him, or you need to stop, grab for that first knot."

"I keep hearing all I'm going to have to do is hang on, but what if I can't do that?" Marcy was still worried.

"If you couldn't do that, you wouldn't be out here. You'll be fine." Casey pulled away and loped on ahead.

"Hey! Thanks for your help," Marcy called. The girl waved without turning around.

Marcy watched as Casey matched her horse's gait to Nickle's and began an animated conversation with him. She had to smile at the memories the scene evoked. Young, horse-crazy girl with a hopeless crush on the man in charge. Was it so obvious to her because she had been down that very trail not so long ago? Yet did she detect a welcome response in Nickle? Perhaps he was over her, or working on being over her, after all.

They turned through a gate and rode into a field populated by heifers grazing or cud-chewing and calves napping. The youngsters looked to be about weening age. As they noticed the intruders, several jumped from their lush green pallets and ran bawling to their mamas, who promptly turned to face the riders with gleams of protective defiance.

Nickle rode back to Marcy. "We're going to gather these and drive them down the lane a mile or so to a holding pen. That's where we'll kidnap the babies. You ride out along this fence until you see a corner. Stay there and keep them from bunching up."

Marcy went in the direction indicated and took her station at the first intersection of fence. The other riders fanned out and began quietly and calmly circling the herd. Marcy fixed her reins as Casey had shown her with plenty of slack in them, and she waited.

The cows moved easily, and Nickle waved an energetic "come on" to Marcy. She caught up with them as the last few head poured out the gate in a loud bovine river. They were going, but with great vocal objections to having had their peace and tranquillity shattered.

"Just ride along back here," the foreman shouted, "your horse knows what to do."

Marcy looped the reins over the saddle horn and placed her hands on each side of it. Just as she was deciding her fears were all for nothing, a large bull calf wheeled and started back down the lane at a hard run. The Chief spotted him the instant he broke from the herd and leaped into the calf's path. With his nose thrust down and forward, eyeball to eyeball with the maverick, he threw himself right—left—back right—farther right—then hard back to the left. The horse stayed a fraction of a second ahead in anticipation of the calf's efforts to sidestep him and make a mad dash to freedom.

Marcy was glad "hang on" had been burned into her brain. The ride was a little like a roller coaster with sharp turns instead of curves, leaps and reverses instead of hills. She was unseated with every directional change, her fingers began to ache.

It seemed to her like the little calf would never give up and rejoin the others. *Where is your mother?* Marcy thought once in desperation.

But he did surrender finally to the Chief's cunning and mobility and trotted back into the herd, casting a few quizzical glances over his shoulder. The Chief relaxed, raised his head, snorted twice and returned to his rhythmic walk.

One of Marcy's first thoughts was "whiplash." She turned her head cautiously from side to side and determined that her neck still worked. Her hands had gripped the pommel so tightly for so long, she feared she wouldn't be able to let go. She flexed her fingers slowly, careful to turn loose with only one hand at a time. Hanging on was important. Being ready would certainly help.

She looked up, surprised to see Nickle beside her. He was trying hard not to laugh, but his recurring grins gave him away. "Well, how do you like riding a real cutting horse?"

"Ouch!" was as succinctly as Marcy could put it.

Nickle lost his battle and laughed. "I know what you mean. But you did a terrific job."

"Job? I didn't do anything but—"

"Yeah, I know, hang on. That's just it. Most people who ride a cutting horse for the first time do one of two things. They either fall off or panic and start pulling the reins, which interferes with the horse. By letting the Chief do his job, you did your job. That was some real riding."

"Thanks, but somehow I don't feel like it was. I didn't fall off because I was afraid to, and I didn't panic because there wasn't time. Next time, I'll probably do both."

He was still laughing as he rode away.

Marcy had to endure her Appaloosa's expertise three more times before the cows and their offspring were closed into the holding pen. Each time, the procedure got easier to ride. She learned to transfer her weight to her feet and use the stirrups more fully. This took some of the wear and tear from her hands and arms.

"Take five," Nickle told her, as the gate was closed on the last heifer. "The Chief hasn't done this in awhile, he needs a breather. We'll separate the calves."

"How kind of you," Marcy sighed, but Nickle was gone. She dismounted, painfully and stiffly, and stretched out in the grass. She was just beginning to feel the kinks start unwinding, when a shadow fell across her face. She looked up at Horse Man towering above her.

"You and your horse better walk around. You'll both get so stiff and sore you can't move."

"I guess you're right," she agreed and rose wearily. They walked down the lane and around the lots. She patted Chief on his neck and told him, "I don't know how you *look* cutting, but you *feel* like you're one of the best in the business."

A lunch truck arrived to serve sandwiches, soft drinks and water to the riders and grain to the horses. Knowing the Chief was accustomed to eating only twice a day, Marcy fed him lightly. She knew he needed some extra energy, but she didn't want to make him sick. She unsaddled him and settled close by with a cold roast beef sandwich and a Coke.

Casey plopped down beside her. "How are you making it?" she asked, reaching for the potato chips.

"Okay, I guess," Marcy answered.

They ate in silence for awhile, then Marcy asked, "Are we going to drive the calves back to the arena?"

"Gosh, no!" Casey almost choked. "We'd never get those little beggars that far as hard as they'll be looking for their mothers. They'll be driven up that chute over there onto a cattle truck and hauled over."

"That's a relief," Marcy admitted. "I feel kind of sorry for the calves, though."

"They're all ready to be weaned, and this is the easiest way. What's sad is when you only have a few cows, and the weanlings come on one at a time. He's not only separated from his mother, he's all by himself. These get a lot of comfort from each other."

"What's the schedule for this afternoon?"

"We'll drive these heifers back and pick up twelve or fourteen steers on the way home."

Marcy's relief was short-lived. "Won't the mothers be as unhappy as the calves?"

"Yes," Casey seemed unperturbed, "but they're not as quick and slippery."

Marcy finished her sandwich and tried not to dread the upcoming ride. In a roundabout sort of way, she was enjoying it. It was without a doubt the hardest riding she'd ever done, and she was still nervous about making mistakes but it was an adventure.

As if reading her thoughts, Nickle walked up and inquired, "Can you hold out for more of the same the rest of the day?"

Not and live, Marcy thought. "Sure," she said.

The return trip was a carbon copy of the morning, except the weather was hotter and drier. She lost count of the irate mothers or disgruntled steers Chief had to run down and turn back. While each performance of that duty racked her whole body with pain, she could not suppress her admiration for her mount.

The drive ended at the arena behind the lodge about an hour before sunset. The riders drifted away, looking frazzled and used up, but content with a hard job done and done well. Nickle's profuse thanks and praise of each departing hand indicated to Marcy why he was so good at his job.

She unsaddled the Chief and was brushing him when Nickle came into the barn. "Go on, Marcy, I'll finish him up and feed him."

"Thanks Nickle, but I'm okay. I can do it."

"You did a great job out there, lady. I have to hand it to you. You're a real trooper."

"Thanks." She wanted his words to make her feel proud, but she was too tired to feel anything. "Say, Nickle . . ."

He was currying his buckskin with a vigor Marcy envied. "Yeah?"

"Did you put me where I wouldn't have to do much? I mean, was I in easy places? What I'm trying to say is, was I where a beginner should be? If this was a beginner's job, deliver me from ever becoming a pro!"

Nickle laughed and said, "To tell the truth, you rode in important places all day. If you'd been a hand on this ranch for years, you probably wouldn't have seen any more action that you did today."

"What? How in the world could you afford to put me—"

"Simple," he explained, "you were on the best horse. To tell the truth again, if you hadn't agreed to come along this morning, I would have had to borrow your horse."

"But what if I had fallen off every time? What if I had decided not to stay? What if I had cut the first calf and come home?" Those same questions had been alternatives she had seriously considered, at one time or another, earlier in the day.

"You would have had to swap horses with somebody."

"Good ol' Chief is really that important to cow work, huh?"

"Yep."

"Who usually rides him for jobs like that?"

"Horse Man, when he's here, or Cole or one of the hands from the other barn."

Marcy fell silent. She looked long and thoughtfully into the horse's big eyes. His quiet nature and eager acceptance of human affection were reflected in those brown orbs. But his intelligence, talent, and enthusiasm for his work were traits that lay hidden deep in his big equine heart.

The degree to which some animals developed loyalty toward human beings never ceased to amaze her. She wished, as she stroked his neck lightly, there was some way she could make him understand what she felt for him. He was trusted, highly esteemed, and loved. Loved very deeply.

Marcy was stirred from her thoughts by the noise of grain being dumped into boxes. Naturally, the sound did not escape the attentions of a buckskin and a roan Appaloosa, both of whom nickered hungrily.

"Come and get it, boys," Nickle called.

Marcy led the Chief to his stall door and slipped off his halter. He jumped over the sill and trotted and few steps across to his feed box. "Where does he get the energy?" she marveled.

"You've got to understand," Nickle put on an

expression of patience and amusement, "today wasn't as hard on most of us as it was on you. Ol' Chief Joe has seen the day, and probably will again, when he'd do that all day long, every day, for weeks at a time."

Marcy felt a twinge of sorrow and regret that she wouldn't be here to share in those days. But that inner twinge lived only briefly in the body burdened with many other twinges more demanding. "Oh, my aching . . . me." she moaned.

Nickle laughed again. "Go home. Fill your tub with water as hot as you can stand it, and soak for about an hour. You'll live. I personally guarantee it."

"Thanks," Marcy answered, with a notable lack of conviction. She waved a weak good-bye and trudged painfully toward Bunkhouse Number Three. She presumed her knees would, sooner or later, realign themselves with her ankles, but for now, they seemed to be permanently bowed.

She stepped into the lodge restaurant to order a sandwich to take to her cabin. As she was leaving, she put her hand out to open the door, and it swung back. Lisa Calloway side-stepped her and turned to give her a thorough and critical appraisal.

"Well, good evening, Miss DeLaney," she said. A sneer of distaste curled one side of her mouth and wrinkled her nose.

For a moment, Marcy felt a flare of embarrassment. Hair dangled around her face in wiry tendrils, stiffened with dirt and perspiration. Her damp clothes still clung to her in places. Her hands were filthy, and she was sure her face was a smeared mess. And this time, though she knew a floral fragrance hovered around the impeccable Lisa, she couldn't smell anything but horse.

Then Marcy's weariness absorbed her embarrassment like a sponge, and she gazed cooly back at her. It didn't matter that Lisa looked as fresh and desirable as a newly opened blossom. It just didn't matter at all. "Good evening, Miz Calloway," she replied, and went on through the door.

"Oh, Miss DeLaney," Lisa called with showy formality

"Yes?"

"I hope you have a nice evening."

The walk to her quarters were filled with thoughts about Lisa. What did she mean by that? Doesn't she ever sweat? Does she stay immaculate even when she is handling her horses? Probably. Somehow, Marcy figured she would manage it.

Marcy let herself in and set her sandwich bag on the dresser. As she sat down to pull her boots off, she noticed an envelope on the floor, just inside the door.

She wiggled her toes in the luxuriously cool air, then went over and picked it up. It was addressed simply "M. DeLaney." She sat down wearily on her bed and opened it. She unfolded a newspaper clipping and stared, uncomprehending, at the headline. "Calloway-Treece Engagement Announced."

CHAPTER 8

HER SENSES WERE SO DULLED by fatigue, its content and purpose came to her slowly. She read carefully.

Lisa Calloway, prominent local businesswoman, will wed Tolbert Treece, owner of Florida's famed Coquina Ranch.

Ms. Calloway, daughter of the late Mr. and Mrs. Horton C. Calloway and granddaughter of the late Mr. and Mrs. Clinton Calloway, is the founder and president of Sun Country Travel Corporation. Her grandfather, Clinton Calloway, was for many years one of the leading cattle barons of the state.

Mr. Treece is the son of Mr. and Mrs. Driscoll T. Treece of Atlanta, Georgia.

A spring wedding is planned.

So this was what she meant by hoping I'd have a nice evening, Marcy realized. She felt nothing but a numbness that a moment ago she resented.

Now, she welcomed it. It was an effective immunization against truths to be understood and decisions to be made. Like a robot, she bathed and fell into bed. Sleep consumed her before her mind had a chance to return to the clipping, the method of delivery, the man she loved and the brunette beauty who had him now. She could only trust God to know the depth of her need and begin the healing process.

Marcy awoke, fighting her way to consciousness through a heavy sadness. It was a conglomerated gloom, a complicated melancholy she sorted through, as she lay stretching her sore, stiff muscles and dreading the day.

She re-read the clipping. Bert was lost again, in a separation less traumatic but more final than the first. She would leave, today perhaps, tomorrow at the latest. She needed to begin rebuilding her heart, after the wear and tear of such a near miss. She knew he was under uncomfortable and unnecessary pressure that her departure would relieve.

Yet, thoughts of leaving generated almost as much unhappiness as did the truth about Bert and Lisa's engagement. A spring wedding could mean any day now, or that it had just recently occurred. She had grown deeply attached to Chief Joseph, and the prospect of never seeing him again was painful. She had fallen head over heels in love with the beautiful, romantic, sun-drenched Coquina Ranch. It was a wonderland, a dream place to be, and now, she must awake, rudely and fully, from the dream.

She would miss Nickle, too. He had quietly but quickly become a good friend.

And she would miss Bert. But hidden deep, buried under folds and folds of sorrow, was a neatly wrapped little package of relief. No more wondering and guessing. No more analyzing motives or reviewing behavior. With the misery came a back-handed sense of peace.

Marcy climbed slowly out of bed. She knew the only way to restore flexibility to her protesting joints and mobility to her cramped muscles was to force them into activity. She pulled on a pair of pink Levis and a tee shirt with tiny pink flowers on it. She tied her hair back with a pink and white grosgrain ribbon.

She had little appetite for breakfast, but got a cup of coffee and wandered toward the barn. There was little purpose to her walk, less excitement for her destination. In her mind's eye, the roan gelding was crunching up the last of his morning grain or tugging lazily at a wad of hay. She blinked rapidly and swallowed hard. This was going to be a difficult day, and starting it by crying wouldn't help a bit.

On her way past the arena, Marcy noticed how drastically it had changed in preparation for the rodeo. Bleachers had been erected along both sides and around one end. A small white room perched on stilts midway down one side. She leaned on the fence to watch cowboys wielding hammers, and saws instead of ropes and reins.

Jesse saw her, yelled, "Break time!" and trotted over to where she stood. "Aah, good morning, my lovely. You are a vision in pink."

The expansiveness that was young Jesse Cole was lost on Marcy this morning. "Hi, Jesse," she replied. "When did all this happen?"

"Yesterday, mostly. While us *good* cow-pokes," he punctuated his bragging with a rough elbow jab, "were out rounding up the stock, the manual labor was working here."

Marcy had to smile. "You mean they built bleachers and everything in one day?"

"The bleachers and two-by-eights that go on a frame are put together with bolts. The announcer's stand is sort of pre-fabricated. We take it down and put it up the same way every year. So there's not really much building to it."

Marcy nodded.

"Well, guess I'd better get back to work. If I hear of any cattle drives needing a hand, I'll call you."

"Don't do me any favors!" Marcy said and moved on.

Nickle was stepping out of the feed room as she walked into the barn. "Morning," he called.

Marcy waved and went straight to Chief's stall. He nickered and offered his nose for the customary stroking. "Oh, I'm going to miss you," she said.

"Miss him? Where's he going?" Nickle had approached soundlessly, and his words startled her. She looked at him for a long moment, then returned her attention to the horse. "He's not going anywhere. I am. I'm leaving."

"Leaving! Why?" Nickle sounded astonished "I thought you were here for a month."

"I thought so, too. But I think it would be best—"

Nickle didn't wait for her to finish. "Don't you like it here? Was it that ride yesterday? Was it something I said? Oh, Marcy, if it was, I—"

It was her turn to interrupt. "Hey, slow down! One question at a time. First, of course it was not something you said. You've been wonderful. And yes, I like it here. No, I *love* it here. And while I admit it'll take me a few days to get over my first round-up, I'd do it again in a minute. I wouldn't let a little thing like a ruined body run me off."

"Then why?" The foreman looked distraught.

"I've just been thinking. Maybe I'd better get on home and start job hunting. I'm beginning to question the wisdom of lolling around down here like a wealthy person while my career is in a holding pattern. I'm afraid if I let it circle too long, it might run out of fuel and crash." She saw that Nickle was searching her face, looking deep into her eyes and seeing behind her words. She looked away.

"I'm a little uneasy about my apartment, too. I haven't heard from the girl who's staying there and—"

"Marcy," Nickle said gently.

Ignoring him, she continued, "—I'm not sure she was the best choice to—"

"Marcy," his voice was more insistent.

This time she stopped talking and looked at him.

"Something has happened. What is it? Or should I say, 'who' is it?"

"Nickle, don't. Please. You're a good friend, but you wouldn't understand. You don't realize how difficult, in some ways, things have been for me here. I'm asking you not to make this any harder than it is."

He laid his hand on her shoulder. When she tried to look down, he tilted her face upward. Marcy felt as if he were peeling away her protection, her tailor-made armor, layer by layer. Any minute now, the raw edges of her emotions would be bared.

"You're right. I probably wouldn't understand," he began with an affection that burned in Marcy's eyes. "I don't know the whole story about you and the boss man. Therefore, I don't know what being here has been like for you. But there are some things I do know. For instance, the man is more rattled than I've ever seen him. And there is someone on this ranch whose sole purpose in life seems to be making everyone around her miserable. Don't let her get to you.

"I know something else, too. You're crazy about rodeo, and you arranged your whole vacation around ours. I'm afraid you'll really feel like you cheated yourself, if you don't stay. It starts day after tomorrow and goes on for three days. When it's over, if you still want to leave, I won't say another word."

"I don't know, Nickle," her voice was unsteady.

"Please, Marcy, give us one more chance. And give yourself the chance to see one heck of a good rodeo," he added.

Marcy offered a weak, trembling smile. Her eyes brimmed, and her lips quivered as the words came out in a hoarse whisper, "Couldn't you at least have told me they were—"

"Hel-lo-o-o!" a voice from the doorway startled them both.

The massive, raven-haired bulk of Horse Man swam into focus, as Marcy blinked rapidly. She stepped quickly into the stall and pretended to inspect the Chief closely.

"Uh oh, sorry if I interrupted something," he apologized.

"Not a thing, Horse Man, not a thing. Just working a little p.r. on a dissatisfied guest," Nickle joked. "What can I do for you?"

"I had a few free minutes, and I thought I'd take a ride. Can I borrow my favorite steed?"

"Afraid not. Seems he's already spoken for." Nickle motioned toward Marcy leading the Appaloosa toward the tack room.

"Hey, little lady, you've got my horse," he jested.

She whirled and snapped, "*Your* horse?"

Horse Man made a show of jumping behind Nickle and peeping over his shoulder. "Wow! Take it easy, little lady, I was just kidding."

Marcy felt ridiculous. "I'm sorry. I forget sometimes that he isn't really mine. I've hogged him ever since I've been here. If you want to ride him, you're welcome to."

"Wouldn't dream of it," Horse Man said, emerging from behind Nickle. "I watched you two yesterday. If you're still on speaking terms, today, you belong together."

Marcy turned back to the Chief. She brushed and saddled him while the two men conferred quietly. As she led him out of the barn, Horse Man was sitting on Nickle's buckskin. She swung into the saddle and rode away.

She was trying to decide where to ride, when

the Indian came galloping up behind her. "Since you won't let me ride him, the least you can do is let me ride *with* him. And you, of course."

Marcy started to protest that she had said he could ride Chief, but she caught the twinkle in his deep-set brown eyes and knew he was teasing again.

"Let's take the swamp ride," he decided for them.

"Fine," she agreed.

"I don't mean to be pushy. I don't have much time to ride when I'm here, and I don't have a horse at home. I love to ride through Little Everglades, and this may be my only chance."

His smile was wide and friendly. His smooth, tawny features were just beginning to crease, and Marcy wondered at his age. "Where's home?" she asked.

"South central Florida."

"With a name like Horse Man, I'm surprised you don't have horses."

He laughed. "I have Tall Bert Trees to thank for my name. I used to work here, rounding up stock and looking after the horses. He said I had given him an Indian name, so he'd give me one. I've been Horse Man ever since."

It took Marcy a moment to comprehend the Indianized version of Tolbert Treece. She tried to put him out of her mind. "If you don't have horses, where did you learn so much about them and rodeo?"

"I grew up in Oklahoma. I've worked on one ranch or another since I was twelve years old. I started competing in Little Britches rodeos about the same time."

Marcy's curiosity about the man beside her was growing. She wondered how close he and Bert were. Irritated with her boomerang brain—toss thoughts of him out, and they whiz right back—she kept up the small talk. "What brought you to Florida?"

He looked thoughtful, then answered, "A big swamp."

They rode without speaking to the entrance of Little Everglades. Marcy sifted through her own inner conflicts, while Horse Man seemed to deal silently with ancient imponderables.

They had traveled only a few yards past the sign, when Marcy began feeling the mugginess. "It's like a different world in here," she said.

"Have you been on this trail before?" he asked."

"Once. I've been meaning to come again."

That seemed to please him. "Did you see any swamp creatures?"

"I saw something that looked like an eel, but it had tiny legs."

Horse Man nodded. "That was a Congo Eel, but it isn't really an eel. It is an amphibian with lungs. You're lucky to have seen one. They're shy and very secretive."

Marcy felt her sighting was quite an accomplishment and began searching the tangle of roots and grasses for other signs of life.

"See that white flower over there?" Horse Man pointed to a three-petaled blossom lining the edge of the swamp. "That's Arrowhead. It gets its name from the shape of its leaves."

Marcy looked about a foot and a half down the

stem to a bouquet of shiny, green arrow-shaped leaves.

"My people," he continued, "used to roast and eat the tubers, potato-like growths, of its roots."

Feeling a little foolish for not making the connection sooner, Marcy stated simply, "You're Seminole."

"Full-blooded Muscokee tribe," he said with unmistakable pride. "I was fourteen when I learned that the Seminoles were the only southern Indians who resisted relocation to Oklahoma. The Choctaws, Creeks and Cherokees lead the way down the Trail of Tears, but we stayed and fought for seven years."

The dignity of his race and all its members long since gone from the steamy swamplands shone in his face. He spoke as if he were a living relic of the yesterdays that were generations old.

"Fourteen is a very impressionable age, and I vowed then to become acquainted with my homeland."

"How did your parents get to Oklahoma?" Marcy asked.

"Oh, in spite of the hard fight we put up, most of us were sent to Oklahoma, sooner or later. A tiny band of us were able to hide from the troops and stay in the swamps, but the vast majority were herded out West. My great-grandparents and their parents took the long walk."

Marcy was spellbound. She was about to ask another question, when Horse Man pressed his finger to his lips.

"Sh-h-h! Stop," he whispered to her. "Whoa, Buck," he said quietly.

Marcy tugged on her reins. As they stood in the middle of the trail, Horse Man pointed toward the water. Marcy looked in the direction indicated, but saw only a rough, fallen log. She looked at the Indian and shrugged her shoulders.

He leaned toward her and said softly, "Look at the end closest to the cypress trunk."

Marcy shuddered when the "log" blinked lazily and flared its nostrils. "An alligator," she breathed. "I though he was a fallen tree."

"He's waiting for a mink or a fish or a careless egret to think he's a log, too," Horse Man said, as they rode on. "There is a duck's delicacy," he pointed to a cluster of rich blue flowers atop long, green spikes."

"What is it?"

"Pickerelweed. Ducks love the seeds, but people with lakes or other waterways hate it. It'll really clog them up."

Marcy could easily see by the network of roots that crept through the mud how the weed could inhibit free water flow. She was enjoying the self-appointed nature guide and waited eagerly for his next lesson. It came soon and suddenly.

"Whoa!" he exclaimed, and abruptly stopped the buckskin.

Marcy followed suit.

"Let's let that fellow have the right-of-way, shall we?" He was looking at the trail a few yards in front of their horses' feet.

Marcy followed his gaze and saw a ripple of black and yellow slither into the undergrowth. An involuntary shiver seized her. "What kind of snake was it?"

"A Coral Snake."

"Poisonous, aren't they?" she asked.

"Very," he replied simply. "Now you see why Tall Bert Trees, otherwise known as 'The Management,' suggests on his little sign that travelers in these parts stay mounted."

Soon the riders emerged into the bright sunshine and fresh breeze. "Thanks, Horse Man. This ride was a lot better than my last one through there." She was surprised at how her own feelings had improved along the way.

"My pleasure," he nodded. "See you at the rodeo?"

His words pulled a dark cloud out of the sky somewhere and settled it directly above her head. "I don't know. I'm not sure I'll still be here."

"Marcy," he began, with the same seriousness that had come over him when he had spoken of his heritage, "you can't miss the rodeo. Tall Bert Trees puts on one of the best in the state, and he's proud of it. He'd be awfully disappointed if you—if any of his guests—missed it."

Marcy caught his mid-sentence alteration. Suddenly, it felt to her as if everybody had taken one giant step from knowing nothing about her situation to knowing everything about it. "So I keep hearing," she said, a little more sarcastically than she meant to. "Really, I haven't decided yet."

Horse Man changed the subject, and they chatted pleasantly to the barn. He rode Nickle's buckskin on to the arena.

Marcy unsaddled Chief, rubbed him down and

turned him into his stall. She poured his light reward of grain into the feed box and walked toward the lodge and lunch.

As she passed the arena, she noticed the chutes were being installed. Seeing the buzz of cowboy activity and hearing the heavy clank of metal gates stirred feelings of excitement and anticipation in her. She really would hate to miss the rodeo. She had been looking forward to it for a year.

Marcy welcomed the lodge's coolness and ordered a cold plate of fruits, salads and meats and iced tea. She ate a little nervously, reminded that the lodge had been the focal point of almost all her encounters with Lisa. But her meal was peaceful and uninterrupted.

What to do dominated her thoughts while she ate and during the walk to her cabin. Would she spend the rest of the day packing or pass the afternoon with some leisurely poolside reading and deepening her tan?

Her decision was made for her, and it lay waiting on the floor of Bunkhouse Number Three.

CHAPTER 9

WHEN SHE STEPPED INSIDE and saw the small white envelope on the floor, her first reaction was one of disgust. "Now what?" she said aloud. "A copy of their wedding license?"

She stood over it, debating whether or not to pay its sender the courtesy of opening it. But as she looked at it, she noticed an Appaloosa embossed in the center of the envelope and the ranch's return address. She yielded to its mute insistence and read the tiny, formal card.

You are cordially invited for supper this evening at my home. My car will pick you up at six o'clock. I look forward to our evening together. Sincerely, T. Treece.

Marcy sat down abruptly on the edge of the bed and re-read the note several times. "What nerve!" she finally said. "No R.S.V.P., no allowance whatsoever for the possibility that I might not come!"

While her pride was being indignant, her more practical self was secretly wondering what to wear. Of course, she would go. This was his way of telling her about the changes in his life. She wanted to grant him the opportunity.

There was a flurry inside her she was unable to identify. Excitement? Nervousness? Dread? *Wonder what he would do if I just pulled on a pair of jeans and a tee shirt and rode up on Chief and yelled, "Yeah, whadda ya want?"*

Dismissing the absurd, she set her alarm, and went through the motions of settling down for a nap. As she lay there, with her eyes closed, her mind raced like a runaway train, faster and faster and faster. What would he say? What would she say? Would Lisa be there? Will it be strained? Could it be any other way but strained?

She sighed deeply and got up, knowing sleep was probably impossible. She plugged in her little travel iron, spread several towels on the dressing table and took her mint-green linen suit from the closet. She pressed the tailored blazer of classic Western design—wide, sharp lapels, closely fitted waist and yoke back. The skirt was straight with a deep pleat in the front.

She then soaked in a tub full of hot water, hoping the water would help relax her. By the time she had washed, rolled and dried her hair, it was three o'clock. She decided to try again for a nap, reset the alarm for four-forty-five and stretched out once more.

Not until the alarm jangled her awake, was she willing to believe she had actually fallen asleep. One hour and fifteen minutes until "my car will pick you up." Marcy couldn't remember the last time she had given a whole hour to dress and apply make up. But when she checked her watch at a quarter to six, she still had to put her shoes on.

After slipping on the bone leather heels, she stepped back to get an overall view in the long mirror. Her hair lay in large, soft folds across the crown of her head. The hairline wisps, which she couldn't have tamed if she had wanted to, matched those she had seen in many pictures. "Studied casualness" one designer had called his model's style. "Unavoidable casualness" Marcy had dubbed hers. She wore a cream blouse with a stand-up ruffled neckline. A green velvet ribbon, which matched her suit, encircled the ruffle and crossed under a small brooch at her throat.

In the final analysis, she had to admit she was pleased with what she saw. It was certainly a far cry from trail grit and horse sweat.

When someone tapped lightly on her door her heart suffered a quick spasm, and she called, "Coming!" She collected her purse and opened the door.

"Express stage to ranch headquarters!"

"Casey! What in the world?"

The red-head laughed. "Don't be surprised at anything you see anybody doing at rodeo time. On the rare occasions when Mr. Treece doesn't do his own driving, Jesse usually does it. But Jesse is at the arena, and I happened to be walking by, and here I am. Get up front with me."

"I was wondering if he told you to be sure and seat me in the back."

When they were settled in the plush Mercedes, Marcy noticed what a brilliant, joyous smile the girl had. She was glad she had come. It would make the trip more enjoyable.

"He told me one thing, and I'll bet you can't guess what it was," Casey challenged.

"I wouldn't even try," Marcy surrendered.

"'The keys will be in the car,' he said, 'oh, and Casey?' 'Yes, sir?' I said. 'For heaven's sake, clean off your boots!'"

They were still talking and laughing when the car turned down the driveway toward a sprawling, Spanish ranch house. The red tile roof was like the lodge's, and the stucco walls were nearly obscured by beautifully planned and maintained flowers, shrubs and trees. Casey stopped, and Marcy walked toward the massive oak double doors.

"Good luck," Casey called.

When Marcy looked back, she was giving her a "thumbs-up" go-ahead sign over the roof of the car. *What was that supposed to mean?* she wondered. "Lord of heaven and earth," she prayed, "please be Master of my heart and my mouth."

Marcy rang the doorbell, not knowing whether to expect a Spanish housemaid, a British butler, or a tobacco-chewing cowboy.

What she got was a veterinarian. "Hello, hello," he said amiably, "I'm Dr. Rinehart. Come in." He was toweling his hands energetically. He stepped aside, and Marcy walked into the cool, tiled foyer.

"Bert sends his abject apologies and says he'll

be here in a minute. You are to make yourself at home in the library." He smiled broadly, as if he were accustomed to performing the duties of a valet right along with midwifing cows and vaccinating dogs. He extended an arm toward a doorway.

As Marcy walked into a room lined with oak shelves and countless volumes, she couldn't help noticing the stains on Dr. Rinehart's coveralls. "Is there a serious problem?" she asked.

"No, no. Not now," he said, still smiling. "One of Bert's favorite mares was presenting her foal in the breech position. But we got her turned, and mother and baby are doing fine."

"Oh, good."

"I'm sorry, but I'm going to have to ask you to excuse me. I have another emergency waiting. Bert should be right in."

"That's okay. I understand. You go ahead." She had barely had time to admire the Oriental rug, the leather upholstery, and velvet-draped windows, when a voice echoed her thoughts.

"Doesn't look much like a Floridian's library, does it?"

"No, it doesn't." Marcy turned to face Bert.

He gasped a sharp intake of air, then smiled sheepishly. "You look . . ." He seemed to search for a word he never found, ". . . lovely. Forgive me for not being ready when you got here. Doc and I had just gotten back, and I had a lot of cleaning up to do. I'm glad you came."

"Thank you. I appreciate your asking me," she replied. She felt the stirrings of a peculiar mixture of compassion and contempt, love and withdrawal, dream and reality. There he stood, the man she had loved to the exclusion of all others for her entire adult life. He was so handsome her heart throbbed, so harried and vulnerable looking it ached, and so involved with someone else she wanted to throw the walnut dictionary stand at him. Not for possibly being married, but for letting her find out the way she did.

"Would you like some tea?"

"I think not, thanks," she said. "I'll wait until we eat."

"I'm afraid I haven't been a very good host, Marcy, either tonight or during your whole stay," he said bluntly.

"I suspect you've been as good a host as you could, under the circumstances. As for tonight, don't worry about it. Emergencies happen."

"Yes, they do, don't they?"

Ladies and gentlemen, step right up and get your brand new Bert and Marcy dolls. Wind 'em up and watch 'em avoid the issue.

"I thought we promised not to start off our next conversation with apologies," she reminded him.

"So we did," he agreed, still looking rushed and flustered. He wandered absently around the room and sat down behind the huge desk.

"This is a little formal isn't it, Mr. Executive?" Marcy asked.

"Oh, for the . . . I'm sorry." He was propelled from the chair, as if it had an ejection seat. "Force of habit. When I'm in this room, I'm at this desk."

He joined her on the couch.

"Your house is beautiful," Marcy complimented.

"Thank you, I think so. I can say that because I didn't have a thing to do with it." She appreciated his attempt at humor. "Would you like the grand tour?"

"I'd love it." Marcy was glad to do something besides sit and struggle with conversation.

The rest of the house held typically Florida furnishings. Light, bright colors, lots of wicker and bamboo, terrazzo floors throughout. Each room sported a variety of plants from flowing ferns to potted palms.

"Somebody around here has a green thumb," Marcy observed.

"The housekeeper, Rosalie. I think she's a frustrated greenhouse owner."

A clear, tinkling bell tone echoed down the long hallway. Bert said, with a chivalrous tone, "Dinner is served, Miss DeLaney," and offered her his arm.

When they entered the dining room, Marcy's vision was filled with bamboo and glass. One solid glass wall stood between them and a profusely blooming garden. "What a gorgeous room," she declared, "and that garden is breathtaking."

"We'll take an after-dinner stroll out there, if you'd like."

"Oh, yes," she said, forgetting momentarily the strain they were under.

"That courtyard is Rosalie's pride and joy. One might go so far as to say that courtyard is Rosalie's reason for living."

"It shows," Marcy said.

They sat down to golden-brown Cornish hens and exotic wild rice stuffing. After praying a quick but sincere grace, Bert filled their plates.

Marcy felt herself warming to her host in spite of her avowed intentions not to. His prayer reminded her that the young man of yesterday had been a seeker. They had talked often of Christ and shared their beliefs. She had to push a lump from her throat with the first bite. "Delectable," she commented.

"Yes. Rosalie went all out, tonight."

"Oh?"

Bert looked like a sheepish nine-year-old caught in some forbidden naughtiness.

Through the meal they conversed easily about horses, the food and the house.

Presently, Rosalie, a tall, thin, angular woman with dark hair and round, laughing eyes, appeared with dessert, a light, airy lemon mousse.

Marcy took the opportunity to compliment her expansively on her way with plants and the marvelous meal. The woman fidgeted under the profuse praise, but seemed deeply pleased.

When the dessert plates were empty, coffee had been offered and refused, Bert circled the table and stood behind Marcy's chair. "Shall we?" he invited.

Marcy stepped ahead of him through the sliding doors onto the gravel path. Young, stately royal palms stood in dark silhouette against the vermilion blush of the twilight sky. The calm air held the gentle sachet of the flowers close and low. She felt as if she were walking through a ground mist of sweetness. Her senses were adrift in this floral sea, and it was with some difficulty that she concentrated on what Bert was saying.

"You don't know how sorry I am that you two had to be here at the same time," he said, without preamble. "I was excited when I saw your reservation at the lodge. When she showed up three days before you were to arrive, I thought I was going to have a heart attack!"

"What do you mean, 'showed up'?" Marcy asked. "Where had she been?"

"In Sarasota, tending to her travel agency."

"Is that where she is now?"

"Yes. She left yesterday."

Then this meeting had been built around Lisa's absence, Marcy felt a tingle of excitement, which evaporated. "Bert, tell me about you and Lisa."

Bert started slowly. "Well, as you probably know, I inherited the Coquina from Clinton Calloway after working here for four years. I hired on as foreman, but more and more of its management kept falling into my lap.

"No one lived here at headquarters except the old man and his grand-daughter."

"Lisa?"

"Yes, Her father, the old man's only child, and mother were killed in an airplane wreck when she was fourteen. She finished growing up here. Lisa was a first class flirt—after me, after every cowboy who ever set foot on the ranch. The old man used to shake his head and say, 'She's spoiled rotten, Bert, absolutely ruined.'"

Marcy could tell by the smile that softened his face when he quoted his benefactor what a warm relationship he and the old man had developed. She imagined Bert became the son he lost so tragically.

"She left the ranch to go to school for awhile, then set up a travel agency in Sarasota. She had inherited enough money from her parents to live comfortably all her life, but going into business was her battle against boredom.

"She never wrote the old man. She didn't even come to his funeral. But when she heard he'd left everything to me, she flew up here lickety-split."

Bert steered Marcy into a gazebo she hadn't seen. A candle flickered on a table. The mood and the atmosphere weighed heavily on her resolve to stay at arm's length.

"Let's sit here a minute," he suggested.

"What unusual chairs and benches," she commented, hoping to let in a ray or two of reality.

"Handmade from cypress. Now, where was I? Oh, yes. She started out trying sweetness and charm, but they were so foreign to her, she couldn't keep them up very long."

There's something wrong here, Marcy kept thinking. *He seems awfully cynical about a woman who is scarcely more than a bride. The honeymoon shouldn't be over, yet.*

"Then she tried shameless flirtation. But when she saw I wasn't buying that either, she moved on to something that pretty well got to me. Guilt. I wasn't family. I had only known her grandfather four years. Who did I think I was taking her inheritance? She was going to contest the will. It was her ranch, and she was going to have it! She left in a real huff.

"Next thing I knew, we were engaged. She put the announcement in every major newspaper in the state. After she pulled that stunt, she came back. Apparently she decided not to sue me for the ranch; she would marry it. This time, she was warm and friendly. Being loving was still hard for her, but she did a better job than she had before.

"I decided I could do worse. After all, she is a beautiful woman. She had society and financial connections that could only help the ranch. And could she ever make me feel obligated to her!"

"Bert, that's enough." Marcy's need to hear the whole story was dissolving rapidly in a wash of jealousy and weakness. "I mean, thank you for telling me all this, but now I know what I needed to know. Maybe we'd better get back." She stood up. When she turned from the table, Bert took her shoulders and looked at her with that helpless plea she had seen before.

"Little One, listen to me, please."

She felt her will slipping away. She felt the loss of her resolve, the disappearance of her resentment, the crumbling of strength from her anger. A soft breeze resumed its journey through the garden, and softly tousled his hair. The candle lit tiny, burnished fires in its auburn glow.

"I'm so sorry if I've hurt you. I'm even sorrier if she's hurt you. I don't know what she's done, or what I've done, or what has happened to make you want to leave."

Well, Nicholson Greer, you're quite a snitch, Marcy was glad for the flicker of irritation, but it refused to blaze.

"Please stay for my rodeo. It's very important

145

to me. Remember how I used to talk about doing some stock contracting and putting together a little rodeo someday? Well, I've put one together, and it's not so little.''

Yes, here was her old Bert, animated, excited, remembering special dreams. Here was the Bert she had been hoping to see.

"There has never been a performance here that I didn't wish, with all my heart and soul, that you could be here to see. Please stay, for at least one performance. Then I'll know that the girl who told me I could do it had *seen* me do it.''

She didn't answer. She couldn't. She let her eyes rest on his, until he closed them and brought his lips to hers in a fleeting, feathery kiss.

When she looked at him again, his heavily lidded gaze was exploring her mouth. He kissed her again, this time firmly. Then he pressed her body to his with a strength and desperation that threatened to smother her. No matter. Dying in his embrace was better than living without it.

He released her and cupped her face in both hands. He kissed her eyes, her nose and returned to her lips with short rapid kisses, as if he were sipping nectar from them. He held her close again, but more gently.

At his touch Marcy felt sublime shivers that settled into a continuous trembling. She wasn't sure how much longer her legs would support her, but she knew the arms of steel would catch her when she fell.

He felt her trembling and closed his arms around her tighter. She retreated from his kisses and buried her face in his neck. She clung to him so fiercely, she felt her fingernails sink into his flesh. She kissed his neck, then his ear.

"Oh, Little One, my Little One," escaped through his heavy, erratic breathing.

Somewhere, in the deepest recesses of her sanity, a warning siren began to howl. It was faint at first, but it soon became shrill and persistent. The more he kissed her, the louder it screamed.

"Bert, stop, please." Had she shouted? "I'd better go. Take me home."

He pressed her to him again, and she let him. "Don't go," he pleaded, "Let's go back to the house."

"No, we can't. It's time for me to go."

"Why?"

"Why?" she repeated, her anger renewing. "Because you're . . . you're . . . Oh, never mind, just take me back to my bunkhouse, please."

"Now? Are you sure?"

"I'm sure."

"Well, fine, then, if that's what you want."

They walked without talking back through the garden and into the house. Marcy picked up her purse and waited for him to bring the car around. Her eyes burned, but they felt dry and empty. *I just had supper with a man who told me all about his wife and then tried to compromise her.* The bottomless void within her deepened when she admitted to herself how close he had come to succeeding.

She had never been involved with a married man in her life, and she wasn't about to start now. Not even with one she loved as dearly and as passionately as she did this one. It was that love that kept her from flying at him in a rage of righteous indignation. It was that love that discerned signs of trouble in paradise and forgave him because of them.

He opened the car door for her, and she collapsed limply into the seat. The short drive to Bunkhouse Number Three was made in heavy silence. Again, he opened the door for her, and they faced each other in the pale outskirts of her porch light.

"Will you be staying for my rodeo?"

She could tell he was trying to keep the urgency out of his voice, but it betrayed him. His use again of the words *my* rodeo conveyed to her his possessive pride in it. It was a gift he wanted to give her. Her dry eyes filled to overflowing at how wrong she had been about his not caring, his not remembering. But it was too late.

She answered his question with a question that had gnawed at her all evening. To her, it was much more important than her vacation plans. "Bert, do you love Lisa?"

"Love her?" He looked amazed. "No, I don't love her."

"Good night," she sobbed and fled into her room and slammed the door.

CHAPTER 10

SHE LAY ON HER BED praying and weeping for hours. "How could he so coldly and calculatingly marry someone he didn't love?" she wailed.

But wait, an inner voice said. *Lisa's the cold and calculating one. She made him feel obligated, remember?*

"Then why did he allow himself to be obligated into a loveless marriage? It's so unfair! Why should his goodness and sense of responsibility condemn him to a wasted life? And how, even with things the way they are, could he have so matter-of-factly held me and kissed me?"

Of course, there was no one to answer, and nothing came from within but more questions. She wept harder, but was only partially aware of it. It was as if someone else were crying, and she felt sorry for her, but there was nothing she could do.

Worry, disappointment, anger, and hopelessness welled up in her like a slowly filling water glass. Worry about the prospects of a miserable life for the man she loved. Disappointment at finding weaknesses in his character she would never have believed possible. Anger at life and Lisa for exploiting all that was good in him. And hopelessness, an abyss of hopelessness so vast within her she felt in danger of falling into it. Falling and falling and falling. . . .

The last thing that touched her consciousness was the observation that the unfortunate person was still crying, and she was still unable to help her.

She awoke before sunrise to discover she was still in her linen suit. The crying had stopped, replaced by a dismal sense of unreality and painfully throbbing eyes. She slipped out of her clothes, let her hair down and put on a nightgown. She saturated a washcloth with cold water, returned to bed and draped it across her eyes. She slept fitfully until leaves and sunlight cast a patchwork of shadows on her bedspread.

Marcy knew, the moment she came fully awake, she would be staying for the rodeo. It would be the last act of kindness she could commit for him and the memory of their young, tender, forever unfulfilled love.

Her eyes felt better, but were still red and swollen. She dressed, donned a pair of sunglasses, and stepped out into the new day. She managed a quick breakfast of juice and cold cereal at the restaurant and returned to her room. On the way back, she decided to spend the day by the pool sunning or reading in the shade. She changed into her swim suit and cover-up and set out again.

No one was at the pool, yet, which suited her fine. If she had her way, no one would show up at all. The pool, the day, the world would be hers alone for brooding. Her mind felt like a crumpled piece of paper, and her heart felt like a matted wad of plastic wrap. The paper could, and she knew would, be straightened and smoothed to its original shape, though many creases and wrinkles would remain. She was not so sure about the clinging, misshapen mass that was her heart.

She had barely stretched out when a boisterously good-natured voice boomed down at her. "I say! Champion morning, what?"

"Oh, hello, Edmund. Yes, it's a lovely morning."

"Been down to the rodeo grounds. They're putting up the public address system. That young . . . Cole, is it? . . . is practicing throwing his rope. Seems rather good, actually. I'll have to admit, I'm looking forward to it all."

"I understand it's quite a show," Marcy replied. "Care to join me?"

"No, thank you. I mean, I'd love to, of course, but I came back to the lodge for a stopwatch. They've asked me to help them test the automatic timers, and a couple of contestants want me to clock them dog-wrestling some steers."

Marcy giggled. "You mean steer-wrestling or bull dogging. It's the same event, but some people call it one, some the other."

"Yes, yes! Quite!" Then he added with a touch of awe, "There's nothing like an American cowboy, is there?"

His statement hit a fragile target. "No, there is absolutely nothing like him."

"I'll be running along. Do drop round."

"I might just do that, later. Have fun."

He waved and nodded and sped away like a schoolboy sent on a long-awaited errand.

As the morning wore on, her tranquillity was invaded by a growing curiosity about the arena. The fog that had surrounded her all morning was lifting slowly. Maybe after lunch, I'll "drop round," she mused.

And "drop round" she did. She leaned on a top rail and watched a young cowboy leap from his horse and drag the steer to the ground. "Good show!" reached her from the far end of the arena.

Nickle rode up behind her and stepped off his buckskin. "Glad you decided to stay," he said, and squeezed her elbow.

She looked at him and smiled, grateful her dark glasses masked the two puffy souvenirs of her decision. "Why did you tell him I was leaving?" she asked bluntly.

With no attempt at a denial, the foreman's answer was light and evasive. "He's no real fan of the dude ranch side of this operation, but he always wants to know about unhappy guests."

"He's lucky to have you."

"That's what I keep telling him," he joked, and turned to remount. "Oh, by the way! Keep an eye out for Chief Joseph. Either Cole or Horse Man will ride pick-up on him. And something else I almost forgot. I've been instructed to invite you to ride him in the Grand Entry, if you'd like to."

She hesitated. Was that Bert's idea? "Not for the first performance. I'd like to watch everything from start to finish. Maybe one of the other performances, though. Thanks to both of you."

Marcy spent most of the afternoon watching what goes on before a rodeo. Later, she borrowed the Bronco and drove to town, where she located a bookstore and bought a copy of the *Atlanta Journal-Constitution*.

Might as well get started now she thought as she scanned the news sections then cast them aside for the classified ads. There were several openings available for people with experience in systems analysis, and she circled four. She didn't anticipate any real problem finding another job, but she dreaded the hunt, all the same.

The first day of the rodeo dawned cloudy and muggy, but by noon, the grayness melted away under the relentless Florida sun. Trailers made steady, sometimes heavy traffic into the arena area. The grounds were soon swarming with dedicated cowboys, hopeful cowgirls and hard-working horses. As Marcy ate lunch in the lodge, she looked out over a sea of cowboy hats.

The hours seemed to drag, though she spent some time at the pool, and walked to the barn. The Chief's stall was empty, so she hung around the arena awhile. She soon tired of the hustle of last-minute preparations, so she returned to her bunkhouse to pass the time until dinner and the start of the rodeo that evening.

At supper, she drew bold glances that made her face redden hotly. Nickle came in and joined her briefly, making her feel less conspicuous and vulnerable.

"My, my!" she exclaimed. "Don't you look spiffy!"

"Thank you, ma'am," he answered, dusting his sleeve off and inspecting his fingernails. His pale yellow shirt was in the Cavalry style, with two rows of brown buttons descending its front in a modified "V." It was trimmed with brown piping. His western cut slacks and felt dress hat were identical shades of brown. "Just trying to dress in a manner befitting my important station."

"And what station is that?" she asked.

"I, my dear lady, am your rodeo announcer."

"You are." Why, Nickle, I think that's terrific. I thought coming in from the airport and then again at the barbecue that your voice sounded professional. How long have you been announcing rodeos?"

"Off and on for about eight years. Never quite made it to the big time, though. Not sure I want to. Ranch work is my first love."

"Well, I can't wait to hear you."

The cowboy he had come to meet hailed him from across the room. He excused himself hurriedly and went to join him.

Marcy finished her meal quickly and arrived at the arena early. She staked her claim on a space next to the rail, close to the bucking chutes. Excitement mushroomed in her.

She waved at several familiar faces and wondered where all the unfamiliar ones had come from. The holding area behind the entry gate was rapidly filling up with people in brightly colored clothes, riding horses of all sizes and descriptions. She spotted Chief Joseph, standing sedately in the midst of the hubbub. Horse Man was relaxing on him with one leg thrown across the horse's neck. Bert was nowhere to be seen.

The bleachers filled rapidly, and Marcy was glad she had come early.

Finally, the loudspeaker crackled to life, and Nickle greeted several hundred rodeo fans. "Good evening folks, and welcome to the Third Annual Coquina Ranch Rodeo. I am Nicholson Greer, your announcer for tonight's performance. What you will see here this evening is a sport that was born and bred on our Western frontier. It produces heroes and legends. It's a glory-maker and a bone-breaker. It's a lover. It's a killer. Ladies and gentlemen . . . it's *rodeo!*"

The flag bearers thundered into the arena at a hard gallop, and Marcy felt her pulse quicken.

After the National Anthem Nickle introduced the judges, whom Marcy didn't recognize, and the pick-up men, Horse Man and Jesse Cole. As each name was called, horse and rider dashed the length of the arena, pull to a sliding stop and lifted his hat to the cheering crowd.

Bareback bronc riding was first. Cowboy after cowboy settled onto his mount, nodded vigorously, and plunged out of the chutes. Some were on high kickers, others were on twisters or runners. The first three riders were unloaded quickly. Then came several who hung on the required amount of time to qualify as winners.

Marcy watched with special pride as Chief performed his duties as a pick-up horse. He appeared to have no fear of flying hoofs, as he

155

ran alongside the wheeling broncs to let the rider swing onto his back behind Horse Man. Just as calmly, he chased running horses around the arena to let Horse Man reach over and release their flank straps. He then stood peacefully until he was called on again.

Twelve contestants vied for four winning places. That meant eight cowboys paid entry fee money for the privilege of chewing dust and rubbing sore spots.

Next was calf roping. Jesse was the only contestant Marcy knew and, though she rooted for him loudly, his first throw missed. His aim was good, but the calf shot through the loop before he jerked it tight. He carried a second loop, as did most ropers, but, knowing the times logged ahead of him, decided not to throw it.

Between each event, Marcy automatically scanned the crowd looking for Bert. Fortunately there was little time to let her mind wander. The first steer wrestler had his horse's rump pressed into the corner of the roping box. His hazer held a similar position in the box on the other side of the steer's chute. At a short, snappy nod, the chute man lifted the gate, and the steer charged into the arena. In an instant, both horses were in pursuit, the hazer making the steer run in a straight line, the contestant's horse easing closer and closer to its head. The cowboy leaned out of the saddle and dropped onto the steer's horns. With his heels digging furrows in the sandy arena floor, he halted the steer, and twisted with nose and horn, until the beast rolled over.

Nickle maintained an interesting, fact-filled,

running commentary. Between steers, he told the story behind the term bull-dogging. "That expression," he told, "grew from a performance by a black cowboy named Bill Pickett. He was a hand on the famous 101 Ranch and daily lived up to his reputation as a rough, tough cowboy. According to the legend, Pickett got mad when a bull pulled up and refused to go into the corral. In his anger, Pickett leaped six feet or so from his saddle and landed on the stubborn critter. He grabbed a horn in each hand swung around its neck, and bit the bull's upper lip, like a bulldog would.

"Pickett's 'bull-dogging' got famous in a hurry, and true to the spirit of the American cowboy, others had to try it. Most of them left out biting into the animal's lip, but steer wrestling had been born."

A herd of steers with wrapped horns were driven into the holding pens behind the roping boxes. Marcy knew that meant team roping. She looked forward to watching Jesse and Nickle compete. Several teams had run, when Nickle announced himself and Jesse. He was temporarily replaced by another announcer, ran down the steps from the stand, and leaped on a horse Casey was holding. The next Marcy saw of him, he was in one box, Jesse was in the other.

He nodded, and the steer was set free with the two cowboys hot on his heels.

Jesse threw his loop first, and it settled cleanly around the horns. Marcy could see his lopsided grin, bent by a ball of chewing tobacco that looked bigger than ever.

Nickle moved in and tossed his loop at the steer's hind feet and deftly closed it around both. The steer stood motionless, the judge's flag dropped, the cowboys retrieved their ropes, and the announcer galloped back to his post.

Only slightly out of breath, he announced their time. The crowd roared, and Jesse celebrated on the sidelines with a boxer's victory gesture. "Ladies and gentlemen," Nickle informed them, "the team of Nicholson Greer and Jesse Cole have just set a record for team roping. Their time was the fastest in the history of Coquina Ranch rodeos."

Marcy watched the faces of some fans. How many remembered that Nicholson Greer introduced himself earlier as the announcer? How many realized he had just stepped out a moment to go win an event? She felt sure many had been completely fooled.

Flying red pig-tails identified Casey as she sped around the course in the cowgirls' barrel race. She ran it in good time, and won second place in a large field. There were twenty-one entries, with some coming from as far away as Mississippi and Arkansas.

After a short lull and a comic routine by a pair of clowns, Nickle informed the spectators that the final event, wild bull riding, was next. "This last event," he warned in a solemn tone, "is the most dangerous of all in rodeo. These bulls aren't happy just getting the cowboy off their backs. They're mean and they're mad and they're out to hurt them.

"This is where that long, tall, silly-looking

feller comes in," he continued, more lightly now. "You folks have been laughing at his antics all evening, but what he's really here for is serious business. The life of each and every cowboy who mounts a bull depends on the rodeo clown. Whether a contestant rides eight seconds or not, there are two ways off—jump or fall. Pick-up horses cannot be used, because a bull will charge and gore a horse quick as he will a man. As soon as a rider hits the dirt, the clown moves in to take the bull's attention away from him. Sometimes, a cowboy will get tangled up in the rigging, can't get himself free. The clown will jump in and help unwind him or pull his hand out of the glove.

"Your bull-fighting clown, the man wearing baggy pants and a painted on smile is Slim Holliday from Newton, Florida, and he lays his life on the line for every bull rider out of a chute.

"That little short guy running around out there with a broom is Dexter Stiles, out of Georgia."

Marcy listened to the familiar speech. Every crowd at every rodeo hears it, in almost those exact words. However, she wasn't paying close attention to the announcer's baritone drone. She was searching the bleachers and the cluster of working, milling, rail-climbing cowboys around the chutes. The last event was about to begin, and Bert was still nowhere to be seen. She had not expected to talk with him, but she wanted desperately for him to know she had stayed. She wanted him to see her there, watching his rodeo.

She finally caught Nickle's eye and mouthed the words, "Where's Bert?"

The announcer read her lips accurately and

pointed toward the chutes. He then held up two fingers.

"Oh, no!" she gasped aloud, when she caught sight of him perched on the rail numbered "2" above a huge, brindle brute snorting and lurching behind the boards. Her mind went into a whirl. Bull riding? Why in the world would he ride bulls? With so much to lose and so much responsibility, why would he take the risk?

As the loudspeaker predicted, "We're just about ready to begin this event, folks," her dread increased, and her heartbeat doubled.

"Our first bull rider this evening is a North Carolina cowboy from Deerfields." Nickle's voice filled the air with anticipation. "Rick Hardin has drawn Hurricane Harry, a real twister.

"What's that, Slim? Did I hear what happened to you up in Kissimmee?"

The clown was shouting from mid-arena. Marcy knew such banter would fill the gaps in action throughout this event. "Comic relief," announcers called it, but her tension was mounting with each passing second. There would be no relief for her, comic or otherwise, until Bert was safely off his bull.

"No, Slim, tell me . . . there he goes!" Immediately all attention snapped from the comedy routine to a dirty gray whirlwind spinning and kicking in unearthly fury. The Carolina cowboy dug his heels in and shoved his left hand skyward in a tight fist.

"Atta boy, Rick!" some railbird whooped.

"Ride 'im!"

"Hang on!"

The rallying cries had hardly been given voice before the cowboy went flying through the air. He landed close to the rail, scrambled up it, and the bull passed close by, but out of reach.

When the bull was safely in the corral, Slim began his antics in the center of the arena, but the humor was lost to Marcy, who saw Bert balanced over his bull with one foot on each side of the chute.

"Ladies and gentlemen, next we move to chute number two." For now, the announcer's foolishness was over. "T. D. Treece has drawn Devil's Daddy for tonight's event. He is a local cowboy who has spent several years working hard for rodeo in this area. We wish him, as we do all the riders, a lot of luck with his ride."

How like him, Marcy thought. During the rodeo, *his* rodeo, he was no longer a wealthy ranch owner. He was just another cowboy. She wondered if he had heard any of that. At the same time, she wondered what had become of all the air. Suddenly, she felt as if there was none left for her to breathe. But before she could worry long about smothering to death and before she could get any farther into her prayer than, "Dear God, please, . . ." she saw Bert's hat dip in a "yes" nod, and the bull exploded from the chute.

"He's outside!" the loudspeaker boomed.

Bert's rhythm was good the first four or five seconds, but the bull did a midair suck-back and changed direction. Perilously close to the chute gate, he went into a sunfishing frenzy. As he threw his huge body one way, he jerked his neck and head in the opposite direction. Bert was thrown over his own right shoulder and slammed into the bull's sweating, heaving rib cage.

The clown Slim gave Bert only a fraction of a second to free himself, then darted in. Just as he reached for the glove, the wrap came loose, and Bert fell into the dirt under the battering hooves.

The crowd gasped in unison. The throbbing in Marcy's chest commanded her to release the breath she had been holding since before his ride began. She stood as if her boots were welded to the ground.

Bert was trapped between the animal and the fence. Slim grabbed the bull's tail, and Devil's Daddy spun around and bounded after him. Several cowboys were already at Bert's side, when he leaped to his feet. He said something to one of them, then crumpled back into the dust like an inflated toy cowboy with a pin hole in him.

Marcy's formerly welded boots sprouted wings, as she flew the arena's length and shoved through the quiet spectators bunching at the rail. She climbed through the bars of the gate. When she got to where he was lying, a paramedic was leaning over him.

"Bert?" she spoke, surprised at the calm voice she heard. "How bad is it?" she asked no one in particular, and no one answered.

The man in white stood, took his walkie talkie from his vest and ordered, "Get the ambulance down here, stat!"

Then Marcy saw him. Someone had straightened him out, so he was lying flat and still. His face was the color of wood ashes. "God, please, . . ." she began again. "Bert? Can you hear me?" She laid her hand on his arm. "Bert?"

"I don't think he can hear you, Marcy," a voice from the whispering huddle suggested. She had no idea who it was. "It happened so fast, none of us are sure whether the bull got him or he hit his head on the rail."

"It's bad news when a bull stays that close in," another voice offered.

Someone called, "Here comes the stretcher," and the tight cluster of onlookers dissolved.

Marcy gently touched his bleeding head and helped the attendants lift him onto the starched white sheets. He jerked and made a sort of muffled whine. She reached for him as they rolled him into the ambulance.

"I'll take care of him, ma'am," the attendant said.

"May I go with him?" she asked, once more astonished at the controlled sound that came from her terrified, nearly hysterical self.

"Yes, ma'am." The driver led her to the front, opened the passenger's door for her and helped her inside.

"See you at the hospital," another anonymous voice told her. She acknowledged whoever it was with a nod.

It was all so dreamlike. She heard people she should know, but didn't. She felt there must something she needed to do, but she didn't know what it was. As the ambulance was pulling out, a small glimmer of reality penetrated her shock.

Just before the shrill siren drowned him out, she heard Nicholson Greer, rodeo announcer, say, "We go now to chute number three, where the bull, Widow Maker, is waiting for Georgia cowboy. . . ."

Still outwardly calm, she began to seek the inner quiet that was always hers when she asked God for it. Because of the fear and confusion, she wasn't able to frame a prayer word by word, as she gazed toward Heaven out the ambulance window. Instead, she silently committed the battered cowboy in the back to the greatest Physician the world had ever known, and began in gentle whispers, "Our Father, who art in Heaven . . ."

CHAPTER 11

MARCY HOOKED ONE BOOT HEEL over the bed's low rail and leaned stiffly back against the wall where she had stood for several hours. She rubbed her face, gently pressed her burning eyes, and picked at the black-red blood stains a hasty-washing had left around her fingernails. The black of night never dimmed the white-lighted hospital room.

She glanced at the limp figure in front of her and then at the electronic clock numbers winking below the television controls. It would be five or six minutes before the cowboy in the bed would begin another tortured, unconscious pantomime of the savage ride that put him there. She closed her eyes and waited.

A murmur and gentle stirring roused her from a half doze. Bert's right hand began gathering the top sheet. His long, boney fingers collected a wad and twisted it. When the size of the handhold felt right, he shifted his body left, then right, up a little, down a little. He flung his left arm upward and let it land on the pillow. His gauze-shrouded head nodded, an imaginary chute gate opened, and the bull of his delirium lunged into the arena.

Both knees jerked, and his back arched, as the phantom Brahma gyrated beneath him. On this cue, Marcy leaned forward, patted him sharply on the shoulder and declared, "Hey, good ride, Bert. It's over, you rode him. It's okay, Bert. Take it easy, now, you rode him."

Slowly, the nightmare ride ended. His teeth, clenched against the imagined bone-shattering jolts, parted. A tight frown of pain and determination melted from his face. His grip on the percale rigging loosened, and Marcy straightened the covers.

"Been riding again, huh?" a voice behind Marcy asked.

She mumbled, "Yeah."

The nurse wound a blood pressure cuff around Bert's arm and started pumping. "How long was it this time?"

"The ride?" Marcy asked.

"No, between rides."

"Oh, fifteen or twenty minutes, I'd say. I think they're getting a little farther apart. I think he's listening better, too. Ouch! I bet I have to cut these boots off!"

"Why?" the nurse asked over the sound of air hissing out of the cuff.

"I've been standing here so long, my feet are swollen to twice their size."

"You'd better get off of them awhile. Sit down here in this chair and prop them up on the foot of the bed. You can get to him fast enough if anything happens. Come here, now, and sit down."

Marcy was too exhausted to protest, and she followed the nurse to a big vinyl chair. They pulled it closer to the bed and she lifted one heavy, throbbing foot onto the corner of the mattress, then followed with the other. "Whew, that's already a relief. I should have done this long ago."

"After you've had them up for awhile, your boots will probably slip right off. It might take a couple of hours, though." She started out the door, then turned. "By the way, his blood pressure is still good, and his color is getting better. I wouldn't worry too much, if I were you."

"Thanks," she said to the nurse. *Thanks,* she prayed to the Lord.

It was another night of prayer and misery, although vastly different from the last one she had spent. This time, she did not plead for whys and why-nots. She spent the time between Bert's attacks of delirium praising God for His grace and mercy, claiming His promises of power and seeking His strength. She knew now that Bert's mending was the important thing. Even if her heart never mended, she would be content with his recovery.

The door closed silently, and Marcy eased her head over against the chair's wing. She knew she couldn't sleep, but she could shift into a sort of neutral gear and idle until she was needed. But clearing her mind was not as easy as she thought it would be. The fake leather squeeked as she settled deeper into the chair. She had no real business being there, watching at the bedside of another woman's husband.

She was surprised at how little she had thought of Lisa. She did not enter her mind at all, until the attendants had disappeared into the emergency room with Bert. Then, she wondered briefly who would call her in Sarasota, if she was still there. Now, after hours of being preoccupied with Bert's pain and suffering, Lisa popped again into her consciousness. Where was she? Did she know yet that he was hurt? Did she care?

The door opened again, and Nickle stepped in. "How is he?"

"The doctor said the x-rays showed no fracture, there don't seem to be any blood clots forming and there is no apparent brain swelling. The scalp cut is not bad, but he put in twenty-one stitches. It not too serious; mostly, he's addled."

"Terrific! It sure looked awful." Before he could say anything else, he wheeled to see Bert sitting straight up, already in the middle of another make-believe performance.

"What the . . . Hey! Boss man, lie down!" he ordered.

Marcy stayed in the chair, feet still high on the rocking mattress.

"Is he supposed to move around like that?" he sounded frantic. "Come on, Bert, lie down!"

"Push him back down, or slap him on the shoulder, and tell him he rode it. That's all it takes. Just tell him he rode his bull."

168

Nickle followed the instructions and Bert quieted easily. Then he looked at Marcy. "Why don't you go back to the ranch? You have to be worn out. I'll stay and if there is any change, I'll call you."

Marcy looked out the window. It was nearing daylight. "Where's his . . . where is Lisa?" she asked absently.

"I don't know. I'll stay with him, now. You go on."

"Okay. I guess I will."

"Here," he said pulling a set of keys out of his pocket. "I'll get one of the fellows to drive you back."

Nickle walked with her out of the room and into a flock of cowboys propping, squatting, sitting, or pacing in the hall.

Jesse jumped up from his seat on the floor. "How's the boss man?"

Marcy was momentarily overcome by this display of loyalty and concern. His employees must think very highly of him, in spite of their differences, she decided. She repeated the report she had given Nickle. They all seemed pleased, and other than the young man Nickle handed the keys to, they all settled back into their various postures of waiting. No one made a move to leave. They would stay, the silent agreement was unanimous, with their boss, their friend.

Marcy felt as if Bert's head injury had left *her* in a vacant daze. She walked beside the young cowboy to the elevator. It arrived with a ping, the doors glided open, and some unseen force propelled her inside. The same ping announced their landing on the ground floor, and she drifted through the lobby into the parking lot.

The cowboy led her to an old Ford pick-up and helped her inside. She listened while the motor growled and finally coughed to life for the short trip to the ranch. Marcy thanked her driver and climbed out of the truck, which immediately headed back toward the hospital. Once inside her cabin she lifted the phone off her dressing table and onto the bed, as far as the cord would reach. She sat down and tugged half-heartedly at her boots. They didn't budge. "I knew they wouldn't come off," she mumbled, as she stretched out on top of the covers.

Marcy awoke as the vibrant blue sky absorbed the last yellow fringes of dawn.

Her weightless, floating mind seemed detached from her leaden body. It drifted from one experience to another, haphazardly reliving the last forty-eight hours. The article announcing Bert and Lisa's engagement, the rodeo grounds, the swamp ride with Horse Man, the embraces in Rosalie's beautiful courtyard, the grand entry, the injured man in a hospital bed.

A shrill noise called Marcy's attention. She thought it was the screaming siren. At the second blast she realized it was the phone. She quickly rolled over and picked up the receiver. "Hello?" Her heart was pounding.

"Marcy? I was about to hang up."

"Sorry. I must have been asleep. Is this Nickle? Is anything wrong?"

"Yes, this is Nickle, and no, nothing is wrong.

In fact, a lot of things are very right. The boss man's awake and already arguing to come home."

"That's wonderful! What time is it?"

"It's only about seven. You hadn't been gone from here twenty minutes, when he looked up at me and said, 'That you, Greer? Where's Marcy?' I waited until the doctor had seen him to call you, so I could make a full report. He says everything is fine, but he'd like to keep him here one more day."

Marcy choked back tears. "Did he really ask for me?" She had to hear it again.

"He sure did." Nickle sounded elated. "In fact, the doctor thought it might have been the change in voices that helped bring him around."

"I'm so glad he's all right, Nickle. Thanks a million for calling."

"Want to talk to him?"

"No, I don't think so. Just tell him I'm happy to hear he's okay."

"Will do. Go back to sleep."

"I'll try. 'Bye."

She hung up and sat on the edge of the bed. Her heart and mind filled with gratitude. "Thank You, God, for being such a loving and listening Father."

She pulled at her boots again, and this time, they came off easily. She changed into a nightgown and turned the covers back. Before she slid between the sheets, she got the number of the Delta Airline ticket counter, and made a reservation for the latest flight the next day to Atlanta. Her plane would leave Florida at 9:47 p.m., little more than thirty-six hours away.

Might as well not prolong this, she thought before drifting back to sleep.

Marcy slept most of the day, ate an early super and decided to join the roar and hoopla of the evening's rodeo performance. This would be her last chance.

She arrived just as the wild bull riding was beginning and stood near the fence, close to where she had been the night before. Spectators were roaring encouragement to a rag doll rider, who was deaf to everything except the bull's angry bellowing and the sound of his own teeth crashing together with every lashing thrust.

The contestant made it to the buzzer, then took a flying leap and sprawled onto the arena floor. When the cow bell landed in the dust with a dull clank, it apparently dawned on the bull that his source of aggravation was on the ground and in easy reach. He wheeled and charged the rider and Slim who had made a mad dash to be in front of the bull. The clown grabbed the fallen cowboy by the belt and shirt, shoved him toward the fence, and ran in the opposite direction. The bull was inches behind him, head down in deadly determination.

Slim dashed down the arena toward a red, white, and blue barrel in the center. Most of the audience laughed good-naturedly, but everyone who understood the danger prayed silently that the clown would make it.

With barely a second to spare, Slim dived head first into the rubber refuge. Before his feet disappeared inside, the big, wide horns rammed the barrel and sent it rolling. The bull snorted, nose in the dust, eyes riveted to the object of his wrath. He pawed the earth, spewing streams of dirt backward with first one forefoot then the other. He charged again, contacting the barrel with a thud heard high in the bleachers.

Nickle was offering the downed rider his routine verbal pat on the back. "How about it, folks, a big hand for Eddie Hawkins, from Dade City, Florida!"

Marcy admired Nickle's ability to take charge and see that the show went on. There was little indication in his firm, enthusiastic voice that he hadn't slept the night before and hadn't returned from the hospital until late that afternoon.

Nine more contestants rode bulls. There were no injuries, other than the customary limping and shoulder-holding. Marcy had no particular desire to talk with Nickle or any of the guests, so she slipped away before the fans began filing out of the bleachers.

She returned to her bunkhouse and began a dismal chore. Leaving out jeans, a tee shirt, her make-up and a dress to wear on the plane, she packed everything else and latched the suitcases. She hoped for one more ride on the Chief in the morning. She settled into bed again and slipped back into sleep.

She awoke early the next morning. She did not feel especially happy, but she was content with Bert's recovery and a new sense of control over her life. The last several days had bombarded her with events and feelings completely beyond her power to alter or arrange. A certain sad peace had settled on her when she had decided to leave. She never expected to have to pick up the pieces of her life that had shattered and fallen around Tolbert Treece twice in one lifetime. But she did it once; she would have to do it again.

The mood in the lodge restaurant that morning bordered on hilarity. It was still filled with the rodeo crowd, whose last performance was upcoming. Boisterous cowboys, some of whom Marcy recognized as Coquina hands, were teasing giggly waitresses.

Jesse left his table and joined her. "Mornin', ma'am," he greeted, grinning broadly.

"Morning, Jesse. I'm glad to see everyone so happy. Special occasion?"

"No, ma'am, just been an awful good rodeo, and the boss man's okay and all. Guess everybody is letting off a little steam."

"You boys really care for your boss man, don't you?"

The youngster shifted self-consciously and looked away, apparently embarrassed at letting his admiration show. "He's okay. We get along all right, except when he lives with us."

"What do you mean, lives with you?"

He was about to answer, when a melodious female voice wafted across the room. "Jess-e-e."

He jumped up from his chair with a hasty, "'Scuse me," and walked toward a blond-haired cowgirl waiting in the doorway. Half the room's population howled, "Jess-e-e."

Marcy laughed and felt less anxious in the light-hearted atmosphere.

174

Later as she passed the rodeo arena, steers milled and ate inside the fence, much like they were doing the first time she passed here on her way to the barn. This time, however, she also passed bucking chutes, seats, and roping boxes, and it would be her last trip to the barn.

She walked straight to Chief's stall. He whinnied when he saw her.

His grain box was empty, but the bottom was wet, so she knew he had been fed. She brushed him, saddled him, and rode out into the sunlight. "I hope you're not too tired for this, buddy," she said, as she reined him to a stop to decided where to go. His answer was an impatient sidestep no exhausted horse would have made. "Good," Marcy stroked his neck, and moved out toward the breeding barns.

The morning was warming up rapidly, promising a sweltering afternoon. By the time Marcy halted Chief's smooth lope at the breeding barns, she was looking forward to their cool darkness. She tied Chief in the shade and walked through the mares' barn across the lot to the stallions'. She noticed Lisa's truck and trailer were gone, and presumed she had sent her mare back to Sarasota.

No one was in sight. Whoever did the feeding must have gone on to other chores, she decided. The rodeo was fun, but she felt sure it disrupted the ranch's routine quite a bit.

She found the reason for her trip munching gaily on a mouthful of hay. "Hi, Bear Paw. How is the ranch's favorite baby?"

The colt left his hay rack and walked to her.

She petted his nose and ears through the boards. "You gave us all a scare, you little stinker." He nibbled playfully at her fingers.

Reluctantly, she left the friendly little horse. She remounted Chief and rode back the way she had come, passing the barn and taking the trail that led to the beach. She already felt a homesick longing for the salty warm air she was tasting for the last time here and the hot sand she would walk barefoot in once more.

She slipped off her horse and pulled boots and socks off. She then led Chief Joseph out into the sand and to the water's edge.

The implacable gulls cried overhead. The sun's rays felt like God's healing balm being massaged into worn, aching places. She stood watching the tiny Coquinas burrow deeper into the sand after each wave robbed them of a thin layer of covering. She was letting the sand erode out from under her own feet, when her horse raised his head and nickered.

She looked in the direction he was and saw the Pinto and Bert moving toward her. She stood motionless.

"Hi," Bert greeted, when he reached them.

Marcy thought he looked pale and was a little unsteady as he dismounted. "Hi. Glad to see you up and around, though I'd venture to guess you shouldn't be riding yet."

He smiled and shrugged. "This doesn't amount to much." He touched what had been reduced from a turban of gauze to a small cloth square secured with adhesive tape over his left ear. "I'd feel a lot worse lying around doing nothing."

Marcy nodded.

"Little One, it has taken me a long time to decide how to deal with the fact that, after seven eternities, the only woman I've ever loved was standing in front of me again. It was complicated even more by having Lisa hovering over us like a starving vulture."

"Please, Bert, I know you said you don't love her, but you shouldn't talk about your wife like that." Marcy's throat was tightening.

"My *what?*" Bert nearly shouted. "My wife? Lisa isn't my wife!"

"I thought . . . I mean . . . the engagement announcement in the paper and all those things you told me in the courtyard, like you could do worse. You said she'd gotten to you with guilt. And she was staying at your house and—"

"Whoa! Slow down," he laughed, and took her face in his hands. "The engagement was all that was announced, and I had no idea she was going to do that. There never has been a wedding."

"But she was living in your house, and she seemed to hate me on sight. I thought—"

"Yes, she was staying in my house, but I was sleeping in the bunkhouse with the hands."

That explained Jesse's remark about his living with them occasionally, she realized.

"And I suppose she did hate you on sight." he continued. "She spent enough time with your ghost, and you were her greatest threat."

But Marcy had one more high hurdle blocking the way to her happiness and she was determined to jump it. Her greatest sadness had been his attitude toward her. "But Bert, you've acted so distant, so remote."

"I know, and I'm sorry. Like I said before, it was crazy having you both here at the same time, and I admit I've handled it poorly, very poorly. I've never loved anyone but you. I regret that I was unable to behave in a way that would make you believe that."

"I wanted to, Bert. You don't know how desperately I wanted to believe that!"

They looked deeply into each others' eyes for a long moment. Apparently bored with the inactivity, Chief nudged Marcy roughly in the back.

"Chief!" she wailed, "You stop that!"

They both laughed. "Let's walk down the beach, and maybe Ol' Nosey will be happier," Bert suggested.

"I couldn't stay mad at him long," she confessed. "He's the most wonderful horse I've ever known."

"He's yours."

"What do you mean he's mine?"

"Just that. I'm giving him to you. From this moment on, he is officially your horse."

"Oh, that would be more marvelous than I could ever say, and it's generous of you, but I can't accept him."

"Why not?" His smile faded.

"I don't have anywhere to keep him. Maybe after I get a job, I can find a place and send for him. In fact"—now was as good a time as any to tell him—"I'm leaving tonight. I thought I'd better get home and start looking for work."

"Have you ever thought of ranch management?" A sly grin sneaked onto his face.

She could only look at him, her mouth open in confusion and disbelief.

"I understand you are a top cowhand. And you're pretty good at diagnosing sick colts. Besides, I'm losing my foreman, and I'm already short-handed."

"Losing your foreman? Where is Nickle going?"

"He wanted to tell you, but I guess it's all right if I do. He's going to marry Casey and run off to Texas. Remember when those Texans flew in to buy some cattle? Seems they nearly doubled Greer's salary to come be foreman on their two thousand acre ranch. It is a great opportunity for him, and I don't begrudge him the move in any way. But I'll be losing my best hand and be needing plenty of help."

"I'm glad he and Casey got together. She really cares for him."

"He and I talked all day yesterday, before they let me out of the hospital. It was a day for coming to grips with life, you might say. I convinced him to take the new job and he convinced me that I didn't owe Lisa Calloway anything, least of all my life."

Good ol' Nickle, Marcy thought.

"So, when I got home, I sent her belongings— lock, stock, and brood mare—back to Sarasota."

"Bert, I'm so sorry I jumped to all the wrong conclusions. I've judged you so unfairly."

"Don't worry about it. I made plenty of

mistakes, myself. I was afraid I'd ruined everything, that night in the courtyard. You must have thought I was a no-good two-timer."

Marcy giggled. "That's exactly what I thought."

"Now that we have everything straight and all misunderstandings out of the way, we'd better get back."

"Oh? Well, okay." Marcy was a little surprised, but the expression on his face looked amused.

They got on their horses and rode back to where she had left her boots. She sat in the sand, dusted off her feet and tugged them on. When she stood up, Bert swallowed her up in his arms then pushed her to arm's length and held her there.

"You see, today's rodeo performance is this afternoon instead of tonight, and you need to get your horse back for his pick-up duties."

She gasped, "I forgot that!"

He placed a finger on her lips and went on. "Besides, I have to make arrangements for a special intermission activity."

"What is it?" she was curious.

"Well, you know the man who gives the invocation at the beginning of each performance is the pastor of my church. And as far as I know, there has never been a wedding ceremony performed in the middle of a rodeo arena between calf roping and steer wrestling."

With a squeal of pure joy Marcy sprang up and clutched Bert around the neck. Laughing, he hugged her to him tightly. "Do you know anyone who would be willing to participate in such an off- beat ceremony?'' he teased.

"I do! I do!" she cried, as they clung to each other under a whispering palm. "But darling, we couldn't possibly! Not this afternoon! What about a license and family and—"

Bert's laughter interrupted her. "I know we can't. That was just craziness. But I never want you out of my sight again for long. I want everything as nearly perfect as we can make it. And, yes, before you ask, I agree. We must be married in church. I don't care whether it's here or Atlanta. God will smile on us wherever we are."

"Yes, He will," Marcy answered. "Bert?"

"What is it, Little One?"

"I can never thank God enough for returning you and your love to me. I would like for us to sort of pledge our lives to Him. Right here. Right now."

"Okay." Bert's eyes were brimming with tears. "I'd like that."

Marcy squeezed both his hands tightly, and their bowed heads touched. Quietly, she revised a single line from one of her favorite Psalms, "Unto You, O Lord, do we commit our lives."

ABOUT THE AUTHOR

KARYN CARR is the prolific author of five books and numerous magazine articles, and combines her love of writing with photography in a course she teaches at the University of Tennessee.

A Letter To Our Readers

Dear Reader:

Pioneering is an exhilarating experience, filled with opportunities for exploring new frontiers. The Zondervan Corporation is proud to be the first major publisher to launch a series of inspirational romances designed to inspire and uplift as well as to provide wholesome entertainment. In order that we might better contribute to your reading enjoyment, we would appreciate your taking a few minutes to respond to the following questions and return to:

Editor, Serenade Books
The Zondervan Publishing House
1415 Lake Drive, S.E.
Grand Rapids, Michigan 49506

1. Did you enjoy reading JOURNEY TOWARD TOMORROW?

☐ Very much. I would like to see more books by this author!
☐ Moderately
☐ I would have enjoyed it more if _____

2. Where did you purchase this book? _____

3. What influenced your decision to purchase this book?

☐ Cover   ☐ Back cover copy
☐ Title   ☐ Friends
☐ Publicity   ☐ Other _____

4. Please rate the following elements from 1 (poor) to 10 (superior).

☐ Heroine   ☐ Plot
☐ Hero   ☐ Inspirational theme
☐ Setting   ☐ Secondary characters

5. Which settings would you like to see in future Serenade Serenata Books?

_____   _____

_____   _____

6. What are some inspirational themes you would like to see treated in future books?

_____   _____

_____   _____

7. Would you be interested in reading other Serenade Serenata or Serenade Saga Books?

☐ Very interested
☐ Moderately interested
☐ Not interested

8. Please indicate your age range:

☐ Under 18   ☐ 25–34   ☐ 46–55
☐ 18–24   ☐ 35–45   ☐ Over 55

9. Would you be interested in a Serenade book club? If so, please give us your name and address:

Name _____

Occupation _____

Address _____

City _____ State _____ Zip _____

Serenade Serenata Books are inspirational romances in contemporary settings, designed to bring you a joyful, heart-lifting reading experience.

Serenade Serenata books available in your local bookstore:

Serenade Saga Books are inspirational romances in historical settings, designed to bring you a joyful, heart-lifting reading experience.

Serenade Saga books available in your local bookstore: